I0663361

# THE
# WATCHER

## K.M. Rice

WILDLING
SPIRIT

Copyright © 2017 K.M. Rice
Published by Wildling Spirit
Cover Art by Lindsey Crummett copyright © 2017
Interior Illustrations by K.M. Rice © 2017
Author Photo by Alexandra Rice Photography copyright © 2016
All rights reserved.

No part of this book may be reproduced, or stored in a retrieval system, or
transmitted in any form or by any means, electronic, mechanical photocopying,
recording, or otherwise, without express written permission of the author. To obtain
permission to excerpt portions of the text, please contact the author at
KMRiceAuthor@gmail.com

All characters and events in this book are fiction and figments of the author's
imagination. Any similarity to real persons, living or dead, is coincidental and not
intended by the author.

ISBN: 978-1-947944-03-9

*For the quiet ones who find the strength to rise.*

# Chapter One

I am the rabbit's child. The acorn and the thistle down. I am Draven Who Does Not Speak. I am the one who has seen.

**Five**

WE ARE all by the well. A group of girls are singing a chant and clapping their hands together in time with the beat.

> *"His name is Draven*
> *And he is a craven.*
> *His name is Draven*
> *And he is a craven."*

Two boys dance around me, laughing and giggling as they dart their hands out to prod my back. Every time I whip around to face them, they are behind me again. The girls continue to sing. One has red hair and one has brown. I don't know their names because they have never spoken to me before. I don't know how they know mine.

> *"His name is Draven*
> *And he is a craven."*

"Go ahead," one of the boys taunts. "Hit me."

I spin about to face him but he's already gone. The second boy pinches my side. I fling an arm out to try to stop him but he hops away.

> *"His name is Draven*
> *And he is a craven!"*

The girls are giggling as they chant but they aren't even looking at me. I don't understand how I am part of their game. I don't understand how this is a game at all.

> *"His name is Draven..."*

One of the boys shoves my shoulder so hard that I stumble. I could catch myself but I land on my knees. Maybe if I'm smaller they will leave me alone. He cackles.

> *"And he is a craven..."*

The girls' hands are slapping out a beat. The boys continue to laugh. The sun is so terribly bright and hot and everything is so loud.

Loud.

The trees are never this loud. The trees are gentle when they speak. I want the forest. But I must wait for my mother by the well as she bade me.

Covering my ears, I curl up and close my eyes. The girls continue to sing. The boys throw rocks that make my skin sting.

I don't understand.

I don't understand.

Much later, after my tears have dried, I'm back at home. Papa is resting on a stump, smoking a pipe and whittling, enjoying the sunlight now that it's setting and not so hot. Mother asked me to collect eggs but I am paused halfway between the house and the coop next to the barn. Paused because the sunlight is cutting into the trees just beyond where my papa sits on a stump. The pines are tall, thin, and beautiful. The light catches not only on their needles but on the many little spiders' webs woven between them. They sparkle like gold.

Papa lets out a quiet huff that is his way of laughing. He watches me with a smile. As soon as he sees me notice, however, he pretends he was only ever focused on his wood. He likes to play a game while watching me by pretending that he is never actually doing it, but I know he is.

The strands of shimmering thread among the needles look so beautiful that I just have to get closer. I step past my papa and feel the pressure of the fallen, brittle needles beneath my bare feet as I step on them. A soft, warm breeze pushes at my back. The pines are so beautiful. They smell so sweet. So sweet that I cannot stop walking into them, even though I can't see the spider's silk anymore. Even though it's getting darker and darker the further in that I step. Even though my father's knife has stopped making scraping sounds.

In the distance is a woman wearing a long white gown. Her brown hair falls over her shoulders. She watches me from the darkness. I often see her in moments like this when I'm not expecting to. She is waiting for me. She is my Watcher.

"Draven."

My papa's voice hisses at my ear, his hand firm on my shoulder.

"You know you aren't allowed in the woods."

"Papa..." I whisper.

When he doesn't respond, I peer up at him. His dark blue eyes are scanning the forest. I know he is looking for any sign of a boar because he never sees her. With a huff, he hoists me into his arms.

"This doesn't look like collecting eggs to me, son."

He tickles my side and I laugh as he carries me back towards the coop. Over his shoulder, I can see that she is still watching me.

"Papa?" I ask once we're near enough to the coop to hear the clucking of the hens, excited by our approach, hoping for food. "What is a craven?"

"Where did you hear that?"

I rest my cheek on his shoulder and inhale the suede of his vest against the sweat of his tunic and the skin beneath. It isn't nearly as pleasant a scent as the pines, but it is his, and he is mine. It's enough of an answer to my question.

## Six

I AM able to climb trees taller than our house. So tall that Mama shouts at me to get down every other day. I never get in trouble, though. Climbing the trees around our house keeps me out of the woods, I heard her say to Papa one day. So she lets me do it. They both do.

Today I'm so high up that I can see the beginnings of the village in the distance. Morrot. Two sheep are trotting along, one after the other, heading down the main gravel road, past the houses. I know they have escaped from somewhere because today isn't Market Day and no one is leading them.

I am happy I don't live in the village. Even from up here and over here it's too noisy over there. Distant shouts and laughter and now the bleating of the ewes. The bleating I don't mind, however. It's the people who I mind.

Our chickens are soft and I know when and why they peck me. I can cluck to them and croon and make them cock their heads and talk back. The spiders and rats and mice in the barn follow patterns. The spiders build webs on the windows and in the corners. The rats run along the rafters and walls. The mice only scurry out into the

4

open to stuff grain into their cheeks then dart back into the shadows.

But a person... a person is the most confusing animal there is.

Sometimes other children want to play chase games which I love. I am fast. I always win. Other times they want to play games that hurt. I never know which game we will play, so I would rather not play with them at all.

Mama tells me that it's important for me to have friends that don't have feathers or fur. I don't understand what is important about it at all. As soon as we arrive in the village, the people we meet say hello. They want me to talk. They say and do things to try to make me talk. Sometimes I want to speak, but when their faces are strange I cannot catch my letters. It's like they all turn into bees and take flight and there is no catching bees. Everyone knows that.

I can talk to Mama and Papa just fine. They don't frighten away my bee-letters. But every time a strange face twists when they hear me whisper to my Mama instead of to them, the bees fly a little bit farther away. I let them.

After all, bees should be free.

### Seven

---

I CAN'T BREATHE. Aiken has me pinned under him with his knees on my shoulder blades and a hand on the back of my head, forcing my face into the mud and manure. I suck in a mouthful of filth instead of air. Panic darts through my limbs. I'm not even sure if I can move them anymore. I stopped trying a while ago. The sensation makes me feel as if I am leaving my body. As if my spirit is starting to detach from my fingertips and toes, recoiling from my arms and legs while the other children continue to chant and shout. I wonder if I'm about to die.

Aiken's voice booms above me like the low rumble of thunder. It never used to be this deep but he's huge now. There are no words. Only his weight shoving my spirit out. He is the blacksmith's apprentice and is thicker than the rest of the older boys. Twice the size of me. No one could pull him off me if they tried.

But no one tries. No one ever tries for me. I am just a shadow of a boy. I heard my father say it the other night by the fire when he and my mother thought that I was asleep.

"He's not like the others," his deep voice had said. "He is but a shadow of a boy."

A shadow... I'm slipping into the darkness of my shadow as my spirit departs.

My face is yanked out of the mud and my scalp burns. Aiken has lifted my head up with a fist full of my hair. I suck in a wheezing gasp that makes my arms and legs burn. My spirit is still there, after all. After hauling in another breath, I open my eyes. They sting from the grit that is now in them.

I can see the red of Megan's hair shining in the overcast light as she laughs over something her friend Prudence says. Neither will help me. I can see Aiken's little brother who is my age, Sven, but his face is tight and his eyes even tighter. If he steps in, Aiken will turn on him, too.

"Sorry," the rolling thunder of Aiken's voice says as the air helps me understand his words again. He pulls my head up a bit more from the mud. "All you have to do is say that you're sorry."

But I can't say it. I still can't even move my arms. I need more breaths. And even as I take another, I know that I can't speak. I can't speak because the letters of my words are like a startled swarm of bees darting about inside my chest and I don't know how to calm them. I don't know how to order them into their hive to use them. Not right now. Not when they're so agitated.

Megan snorts and covers her mouth when I don't speak.

"Come now, Draven," her friend Prudence says, resting a hand on her hip as if she were her mother. "It's only one word."

"Surely you can manage at least one," Aiken taunts by my ear, his voice cracking because he has recently begun to grow a mustache.

I work my jaw. I cough out mud. But the bees inside only threaten to sting when I try to make them do what I need.

Then I see it. A swish of brown robes several yards away. Elias is stepping out of his library, walking purposefully towards the well. He is our village elder. Our leader. They will listen to him. He glances this way. Long enough to see what's happening. I want to cry out his name. I want to crawl to him and cling to the hem of his robes as if they were my mother's skirts. Until I see it. His lips twist up at the corners. It's an odd little look because he is trying to wipe the expression off of his face, even as he turns his head away from me, but it is a smile. He continues towards the well.

"Fair enough, then," Aiken says. He hasn't seen Elias. None of them have. "Time for another lesson."

My face is smashed back into the muck before I can really fathom what the boy pinning me down had said. I wasn't ready for it. I didn't have time to take a breath. I can't breathe. Muddy water burns my nostrils and pebbles are scratching my sealed lips as Aiken smashes my face down even harder than before.

Everything is hot. So hot. The bees are all stinging me inside, punishing me for letting my letters get so wild. I can't breathe. My head burns. My head. My...

Aiken's weight is gone. I feel like nothing without him. A shadow in the mud. I know I should lift up my head but I can't. It's too heavy and my arms won't work.

Then an arm is around my waist and I'm hauled up so quickly that I flop backwards into someone's lap. Soft hands are roughly wiping at my face, trying to clear the mud from my nose and mouth. I take a deep breath only to have dirt fly into the back of my throat, sending me into a coughing fit. My rescuer hugs me to their torso and I feel the stays of a corset as I lean into the warmth of their body.

A woman. Mother?

She is shouting. I can feel vibrations in my mother's chest as she scolds Aiken. Shaming him. Only the vibrations don't have the same cadence as my mother's words. Her body is too narrow. Her bosom too small. Though I can't make out his words, Aiken has a strain in his voice. As if trying to get out of some predicament. My eyes are burning. I keep blinking but I can only glimpse blurry blobs of color. Megan's red hair and Prudence's brown. The figure of Sven darting away.

Dark hair falls over her shoulder, into my blurry line of sight. She smells like apples. She isn't my mother but I don't care because she is mothering me all the same. She gets to her feet and awkwardly hoists me onto her hips. Only my father holds me like that these days. My legs are too long for coddling, he scolds, even as he does it.

As she carries me, clinging with both hands to keep me up, I hug her neck and try to hide my face there. After a few steps, I realize she's still speaking to someone who is keeping pace with her. I know that voice. I would know it anywhere. I peel my face away just long enough to glimpse blonde curls walking beside us then I squeeze my burning eyes shut once more.

Willow.

I now know who is holding me. Willow's big sister Scarlet who always offers me a cookie when I come to play. I never say no. I hear her asking Willow to bring water and rags. She sets me on something flat with a hand on my back to keep me steady. I don't dare open my eyes but I feel the surface. It's made of wood. Like a table. I hear Willow's bare feet pattering as she runs back in. Some of the water splashes onto the ground.

I hold still as Scarlet gently cups my face by the chin, holding it while she uses a dripping rag to clean off my eyes. It isn't a comfortable sensation. The grit has left little cuts all over. Some of the mud crusts in my nose as it dries and it hurts as I pick it off. I hear Willow laugh at the sight. The pleasant sound makes me smile. She's only a year younger than I am.

When I open my eyes, they are watery but much better. So much better that I want to hug Scarlet. Instead, I hold still as I blink, helping my tears wash away the last of the filth. Both sisters are looking at me expectantly. Their colors are so different but their concern is mirrored on each face. I'm eye level with Scarlet and realize that she brought me to her father's shed. I am sitting on his workbench. He is a merchant. Strange items to trade and that have been traded are scattered around me. Eyeglasses. A set of large horse shoes. Urns of lamp oil. Willow peers up at me, biting her lip and hugging her hands to her chest.

"Is he blind?" she asks.

"No, silly," Scarlet replies with a small laugh, ruffling her sister's hair. "That's the one thing you will never be, isn't it, Draven?"

I shrug one shoulder and pick at a fraying fiber in the wood beneath me with my thumb. The bees are still buzzing about in a cloud. I can't calm them yet.

Scarlet dips a fresh rag in the water and tenderly sets to work wiping at my cheeks and forehead, hair and neck. I peer at my hands as she does so. They are laced with thin red scrapes from the rocks. My neck and cheeks burn a little when I realize that I smell like more than mud. I smell like horse dung.

"I hate him," Willow snips, plopping down on the floor with a huff. "I hate Aiken."

"None of that, now," Scarlet softly cautions as she shifts her attention to my hands and arms.

"But I *do*. Draven is my friend."

Friend. One word. That's all it takes.

Suddenly the bees are quieting in their buzzing, slowing in their flights. I feel them forming the word in my chest as my eyes latch onto Willow's. She smiles, the sea-green of her orbs sparkling with a light that burns brightly within her. A light that reminds me that mud and manure can grow the most colorful flowers.

"You do not hate Aiken," Scarlet continues to her sister. "You hate what he did."

"Yes," Willow agrees. "I do."

"And to think he asked me to Midsummer's Dance...." Scarlet mutters as she plops the rag in the bowl of water and rests a hand on her hip with a small sigh.

I study my skin now that most of the mud is gone. It's golden and marred by small scratches. It will heal. My trousers and tunic, however, are cold and wet, weighed down by the drying filth. I know I should want my mother, but I don't. Because I am already safe. Scarlet has helped my body. Willow has helped my mind.

"Don't go," Willow warns her sister.

"Oh, I'll go, all right," Scarlet contends, gathering up the soiled rags and placing them in the bowl. Her blue eyes are as tight as her jaw. "But certainly not with Aiken."

While they are conversing, I scoot to the edge of the workbench and slide off. I take a few steps but stop, staring out into the pale white square of the doorway and the overcast day. Both girls are watching me, as if worried I will run. I hug my wrists to my chest, clutching one with the other. My skin hurts. I can't repress a shiver that shakes my torso.

Scarlet asks me a question with her eyes. Her cheek and chest and nearly all of her skirts are covered in mud from me. Even some of her hair. Willow has two dark patches on her dress, as well, where her knees pressed into the mud. Because she was there alongside her sister, coming to rescue me. To help me. Because I am her friend.

I take a step towards the overcast sky that I can see through the doorway.

"Draven," Willow says softly. I pivot to peer at her.

Her round face is shy, as if she is also sometimes unsure of her words. The golden brown of her skin contrasts the white line running horizontally across her nose from the sunlight. Her eyes seem like twin jewels against such gold.

"Why did he attack you?"

I haven't thought about this yet. Everything happened so quickly. One moment I was humming to myself, wandering past his hammer and anvil outside of his forge. Aiken had been there, holding something metal in the fire with a pair of tongs. The next thing I knew, the air was full of shouts following after me.

Scarlet turns away from me to continue tidying up and I realize I've waited too long and that they don't expect me to answer. At least Scarlet doesn't. I can feel the buzzing going away completely as Willow gazes at me, so still and calm.

"I touched the hammer," I croak out.

Scarlet spins around to look at me. "What hammer?"

"Tools," I continue, clearing my stale throat. Because I remember now. I was lost in my song. Trailing my fingers over things that looked smooth as I wandered past. I touched his tools resting on the anvil. He told me not to touch his things. It took a moment for his words to worm in past the song in my head. He told me to stop humming like a girl and to apologize. I saw that he was angry then. He asked me to apologize but my words had already started to buzz in a panic over how red and sweaty his face was from the coals. How much his lip sneered, surrounded by his bristles.

"Oh, that pompous ass," Scarlet mutters as she moves to dry her hands on her skirts, only to seemingly notice for the first time that they're filthy. "Pay him no heed, Draven. It's his own self he is let down by. Not you."

Not me?

Not me.

No matter, though. I'm determined not to make the same mistake. I vow to never hum again.

# Chapter Two

## Ten

W illow comes by every day and each afternoon is convinced that my hatchling falcon Lady has grown bigger. I know she's right and that my hunting bird must be growing every day, but I can't see the difference like she can and I wonder if she is just making it up.

"You have to go away and then come back," Willow explains as she cradles the downy chick in her palm, holding her to her chest. "I notice because I go home then come over again."

I bite the inside of my lip as I consider this, peering at Lady, wondering what it is that Willow notices as different. Are her grey feathers slightly longer or wider? Is her beak sharper? Her body heavier?

"I think she just mostly stays the same," I reply with a sigh before flopping onto my back on the old hay.

It was harvested last summer and sends up a sparkling dance of dust into the beams of sunlight. I watch them drift as Willow coos to the chick. The straw bracelet she braided for me on the day that Lady hatched is still on my wrist. Sometimes it pricks my skin but I don't mind. It's just a reminder that she gave it to me. Willow: my best friend without feathers.

Though I am bigger and stronger now, my parents still don't like me heading into the woods on my own, which is why I had to sneak out to collect Lady when she was just an egg. The story of that adventure is Willow's favorite. She often asks me to tell it to her, as if I am brave. One day I will prove to my parents that I know how to hide from both boar and bear. That I can walk the woods without fear. But still, it's as if they worry I will never come back. As if I am so easy to die.

"Then how do you expect she will ever get grown if she isn't changing?" Willow contends, reminding me that she is there.

I loll my head to the side to peer up at the two, the straw itching my back through my linen tunic. The sunlight is catching in one of Willow's eyes, making it pale and seemingly a different color than the other, and I realize that she is right. That sometimes there are tiny changes that happen while people are away. That I hadn't noticed the way Scarlet had pulled back the top half of Willow's hair that morning.

"She'll never be grown," I reply, not bothering to hide my whine. "It's taking a hundred years."

Willow rolls her eyes. "It has only been a fortnight."

"*Forever*," I press.

She ignores me and instead holds the chick into the shaft of light. I immediately bolt upright. Lady's white, poofy body is crested by the sunlight, making her look like she is radiating the dust mites like magic. She swivels her head, her large black eyes set against her grey skin blinking sideways in the brightness.

Willow giggles a little at my reaction but I can only distantly hear her laughter, for it is outside of the sunlight and the magic. She isn't Lady.

I slowly smile.

# Fourteen

## Spring

THE DEER CARCASS seems to be growing heavier every ten steps. I don't know how long it has taken me to carry it from my kill site in the north, but I'm tired. I can smell the woodsmoke from Morrot's cookfires. I know I am close. I just wish I was stronger.

Lady chitters from a branch nearby. I catch sight of her black-capped head as she preens herself. Hunting is so much easier when Lady brings back the game. I can carry a brace of conies or ten squirrels easily. A dozen partridges. A hundred—

I stop my thoughts because they remind me of why I have killed a deer rather than partaking of Lady's usual offerings. There is a darkness in our woods. A black haze that we first thought was a trick of the eye but it's slowly growing. Most talk about it as if it is part of the weather. Something that will pass. A curiosity. I hope they're right. All the same, I'm not taking any chances. My father told me that if I bring back a deer, he'll smoke it so that we can store the meat.

Once back at our cabin, I lash the deer carcass to a tree and set about skinning it. I gutted the buck and left most of his entrails back at the kill site but I have plans for this hide. If I can get it soft enough, I'm going to surprise Willow with a—

"Now *that*," a female voice says behind me. I'm startled, not by her presence, for I heard her light step in the back of my thoughts, but rather by her register. She isn't my mother. "*That* is a kill."

I whip my torso around to spot Megan. She's smiling, holding a basket of wildflowers with one hand, toying with a red tress with the other. The lovely girl looks me up and down, pressing her pink lips together, and I realize that my trousers and tunic are soaked with blood. It stains my arms and hands and is in my hair that's falling out of its ponytail.

My letters begin to hum, agitated by her presence, but I try to soothe them by reminding myself that Lady is near. Even after all these years, even though I am now a head and shoulders taller than her, Megan is still the girl who laughed with her friend while Aiken tortured me. No, it wasn't just Aiken. The jeers and smiles of everyone there tortured me.

Turning away from her, I reposition the skinning knife in my slippery hand and refocus on my work. Hopefully she'll continue on her way past the cabin. Finish picking her flowers. I can't help but cringe when she speaks again. She is still here.

"I love venison, you know."

My left hand holds a wad of fur and skin, ready to yank it down so that the knife in my right can slice through the fat and sinew, but I don't move. The buzzing of my letters gets louder as my thoughts begin to tumble around each other.

Why is she here? Why is she trying to speak to me? There's a trick somewhere. A cruelty. I must look affright. That's it. She is memorizing all of the details of my pathetic state to tell Prudence. Aiken. Anyone who will listen. They will laugh. They will tease. And the next time they see me, they'll—

"I didn't realize you hunted."

Her voice is soft. Though my hands are still poised, I slowly turn my head to look at her. I hunt for a stiffness in her shoulders; a tension at the corners of her mouth that isn't there. Instead, she offers me a slight twitch of her lips. A half smile.

I don't realize there's a line between my brows until it's deep.

When she clasps both hands together and lets her basket of wildflowers slide down her wrist, I understand that she isn't passing by, after all. She is at the end of her path.

Me?

A breeze cuts across us, blowing her hair over her shoulders. I can feel the tension of the buck carcass trying to sway on its rope. Mister, our orange and white barn cat, meows as he saunters across the yard towards me, pausing to stretch his front legs. All of this should have given the buzzing in my chest time to calm, but it hasn't.

Because Megan is the girl all the boys talk about. She has a wide mouth and thick lashes. Each side of her face perfectly mirrors the other, even the arches in her elegant brows. Only her freckles aren't in perfect unison with each other, but that only adds to the charm of her face. When she smiles, her eyes scrunch up and even I can't help but admire her beauty.

So again... me?

Megan shifts her weight and the small smile is gone. She tucks her hair behind her ear and tries to keep her expression pleasant, but there's now a thin line on either side of her lips.

"I can bake," she quietly offers before continuing at a clipped pace. "I'm not very skilled in the kitchen, but with my father being the miller I have plenty of flour. I make mistakes that I learn from and do better the next time I try."

My lips part. She's babbling. Her freckled cheeks have a pink tint. Something is making her nervous. Am I making her nervous?

"Well," she says with finality, her brown eyes no longer on mine. She looks around her shoes as if she has dropped something but she hasn't. "I suppose I should be going. Good afternoon, Draven."

Without so much as another look my way, she walks back towards the heart of the village. The breeze continues as she goes, blowing loose some of my hair. I don't know why, but my skin flushes just as hers did.

I stare back at the deer, tracing the white lines of sinew stretching between the pelt and the meat.

Megan. Came to see me.

Me?

Something rubs against my shin and I suck in a startled breath.

It's Mister. The old cat seems to take no notice of my reaction and rubs again with a high-pitched meow.

## Autumn

My father is dead.
The darkness is spreading.

My father is dead.
Lady is restless.
My father is dead.
Willow.

She held my hand. Everyone else was dancing and making merry at the harvest festival. Living their lives. Living. Living.

But Willow...
She let me weep.
Willow.
She is my friend.

She hears my words without me speaking them. She hears my words even when I don't know what they are.

---

THAT NIGHT at the harvest festival when she comforted me as I wept, I had a glimpse of what it must feel like to sense a spirit. Because I sensed hers.

My body has become thin. Not because I have lost weight from not eating, but because a body is just so breakable. So fragile. So easy to die. Mine is just muscle and bone and skin. So thin. So thin. Through its parchment walls I felt her spirit. Bright and warm. Like a hearth.

I wanted to fall into it. I wanted to die in it.

So I left.

I should not want to die, my mother says. There's so much living to do. She knows my thoughts even though I don't voice them.

So much living... so much living...

Lady chirrups on her roost, flapping her restless wings. We haven't gone out in... I can't remember how long it has been. Days. Weeks? I'm a poor master to her.

I cannot feel my throat. The bees that are my letters are hibernating. Maybe they have fled altogether. I cannot feel my throat because I have no use for it.

Let it rot. Useless thing.

## Winter

SNOW FALLS. It has been for days. Everyone else young delights in it. Making shapes and sculptures from the snow and hunting out their sleds. As if the darkness in the forest has not been growing.

But what do they know? I am the only boy my age who hunts. The only one to spend any time among the trees. The only one among them to have seen it.

I walk amongst them now, making my way through the main street with a boar on my back. People turn to watch me pass and I know that my shoulders are stained with the pig's dark blood and that I'm hunched under its weight, but I would bear any weight for this purpose. This meat is for Willow and her family.

Megan and Prudence are rolling up balls of snow and throwing them at each other. They pause in the middle of their fight, their green and blue dresses bold against the white on the ground. Prudence's gaze darts from the game on my shoulders to the hunting knife on my hip. She presses her lips together and casts a lingering look to Megan.

They are sharing some secret. Probably a joke about my long legs or my matted hair or my quietness. I don't care.

Megan turns her gaze away from me and seems to relax, only to pelt Prudence with a snowball much harder than necessary. Prudence shrieks and scolds the redhead's name, but Megan only cackles.

In a few moments I'm at Willow's door. I knock. Her mother answers with a smile, drying her hands on her apron.

"Good afternoon, Draven."

I incline my head with a small smile. I know I ought to greet her with my words, but my bee-letters are still hibernating. They have been for so long that I have given up on trying to coax them back out.

"My, that must be heavy," she continues then calls over her shoulder. "Jasper, go and fetch your father to help the poor lad!"

Jasper is only four and never listens to what he's told to do unless it means an escape from the cabin. The boy darts outside without even bothering to put on a coat. I glance around for any sign of the girls, even though from where I am standing I have already assessed that they aren't in the cabin.

"Can I offer you some tea?" their mother asks. "How is Gwen?"

I peer at her, staggering under the weight of the boar, and she blinks then twitches her face away, as if reminding herself of the foolishness behind asking me such questions.

Me. The boy who lost his words. The shadow.

Their father enters shortly after and takes the pig from me. I try to hide the way my shoulders begin to tremble once the weight is gone. After nodding my head in thanks, I slip back out. The snow falls steadily now and I jerkily wrap my arms around my torso as I step out into it. I only make it a few yards before I spot them coming out of the woods across the nearby meadow: Willow and Scarlet. They are bundled in their cloaks, their arms laden with firewood. My mouth moves on its own accord at the sight of her blonde curls, and when I realize I'm half-smiling, I fight the expression off of my face. I turn away to head home but she calls my name.

"Draven!"

I can't. She is too bright. I can't.

Then my feet are moving. I walk towards her without even registering my actions. I wait in the center of the meadow. Like a scarecrow in a white field.

Scarlet casts me a greeting smile as she passes. Her blue eyes look all the more sapphire against the whiteness of her winter skin. She continues on towards her home but Willow doesn't. Willow stops. I stare at the ground for the world is suddenly too much. Willow moves to stand before me, crunching the snow beneath her boots.

I can't look at her. Not now.

"Draven?" She tries to catch my eyes.

My name is so soft on her lips that I could almost pretend it was in the wind. My shoulders are hunched and trembling from fatigue. When I remember that Lady is roosting in the barn and not waiting for me on some nearby roof or tree, I lower my head a little more. Because I am growing thin again and can feel her warmth calling to mine. I don't want to feel it. I just want to be a shadow. A shadow...

The branches in Willow's arms suddenly fall to the ground, landing on our feet. It startles me as much as it hurts. My body jerks. Then my body is being wrapped up in hers. This isn't a hug. This is forceful and desperate. Like rescuing a victim from the rapids. I can't move. She hooks a hand around the back of my neck and forces my head down against hers. I close my eyes.

We stand like this for some time. My thinness hums. I'm basking in the warmth of her spirit. So warm that the frost is melting inside of me. I can feel the steady dripping of thawing ice.

They are awakening.

She sniffles and I realize she's crying. I wrap my arms around her and she leans into my chest. She doesn't care that my shoulders are damp with pig's blood. The wind blows, chilling us both, but we don't budge. Then something shifts inside of me, like the cracking of a frozen river. A gasp escapes. I squeeze.

"Willow," I creak.

The bees are shaking out their wings.

"Oh, Draven," she whispers.

"Willow... Willow..."

It's all I can manage. It's enough.

Over her shoulder I glimpse a small animal in the snow, like a brown fox flicking its tail. But it isn't a fox at all. It is hair in the breeze. Dark hair falling over the shoulders of a woman in a white dress that nearly blends in with the white landscape. My heart skips a beat for I haven't seen her in years. Not since I was small. My Watcher. She is too far away for me to make out her features and I am too tired inside to try to even understand.

When I finally part from Willow, I can't meet her gaze. My skin is flushed. I feel so small, as if I were again the boy Scarlet rescued from the mud. Pathetic. But full. Full of Willow's light.

In the distance, the woman in white is gone. I hurry away. Once back home, my mother asks me what took me so long.

"Willow," I reply on my way to the fire.

I pretend not to notice my mother's stare.

The bees are humming again.

# Chapter Three

**Seventeen**

---

The darkness reached Morrot last year. A part of my mind still
tries to tell me that it's dusk, not noon. I fear the day that I no
longer have to correct my thoughts. Today is Midsummer. There are
no bonfires. No festivities. The fear is as palpable as the dark.

Lady shifts on my shoulder. She grows lighter every week. I stroke
her back and offer her a soft coo as I walk down the main street of the
village where people are still out and about. In place of gay chatter
and laughter there are hushed voices and coughs.

The forge is on my right. It has been cold for months. Aiken's
tools lie where he left them whenever he stopped working weeks ago.
I'm taller than Aiken now, and almost thicker. Hunger hasn't been
kind to him. What good is shaping horse shoes when there are no
horses?

I eye the hammer. I am tempted to touch it. To take it. Just to see
what he will do now that I have overtaken him in height. But it would

take too much energy. I have only recently noticed how much energy anger consumes. Like a fire, it feeds on every thought and action. I'm not yet weak, but I am still too tired to feed such a beast.

Passing the well, I hear the clatter of the bucket hitting the stones of the side as a woman lowers it down. Food may be scarce, but at least our water is still plentiful. These days, it's important to focus on what we have, rather than what we don't. I am still wealthy. I have Lady. I have my mother. I have my strength. I have Willow.

Someone laughs and it's such a cheerful sound that it reminds me of the purples of blooming heather. I spot the owner of the voice ahead. Scarlet. She has a shawl over her hair and shoulders to fight off the nip in the air. Jasper is holding her hand and making funny animal noises. She's carrying their large cooking pot so I know they're headed for the well.

Elias steps out of his library and I stop walking. The man stretches his back, twisting it one way then the next as he surveys the village. His eyes linger on Scarlet and Jasper as she swings their linked hands while they walk. From my vantage, I can't actually see his pale orbs moving up and down, but I know they are.

I'm not cold but something akin to a shiver irritates the back of my neck and my spine. As if I had feathers to ruffle. I stare at Elias as if my gaze alone could shove him away. Repel him from ever looking at Scarlet or Willow or Megan again. A voice in the back of my head reminds me that I'm being ridiculous and that Scarlet is his pupil. They are close. But I don't see a teacher. I don't even see a leader. All I see is the man who once smirked as I was nearly suffocated in the mud.

My feet start moving again without my noticing right away. I join Scarlet and Jasper at the well.

"Allow me," I offer, reaching out a hand for the iron pot.

Scarlet greets me with a bright smile that seems all the wider given the narrowing of her cheeks from hunger. "Draven. Thank you. I have Jasper here to help."

Jasper is six and small and pale. He no longer runs manic circles around us. At least once a day, I hope that he won't die. He peers up at me and his pinched face looks goofier now than it ever has. I grin and ruffle his greasy hair. He hugs my leg.

"I hope you have been doing your job," I say to him in a firm voice.

He rests his chin against my leg and peers up at me. "What job?"

"Torturing your sisters for me, of course. I thought we had an agreement."

On cue, he darts away from me and starts trying to tickle Scarlet's sides, a feat easier now that she doesn't wear a corset anymore. None of the women do. In times of discomfort, it's only fair that they seek comfort wherever they can. Scarlet bats him away while fixing me with a playful version of a withering glare. "Oh, Draven Lucian's Son, you are just begging for revenge."

I chuckle as I grab the rope and begin raising the bucket of well water. "I welcome it."

Lady ruffles her feathers, as if in agreement.

"She is pricking your tunic," Scarlet observes.

"It's only clothing," I say. I want to feel her while I can.

Once the bucket is up, I pour it into their pot then kneel so that Jasper can stroke my falcon's back. He hasn't asked to yet but I know he will. I can feel the warmth from Scarlet's eyes as she watches us. Though we never speak of it, I know she worries about Jasper's thinness more than I do.

"So pretty," Jasper coos at the bird.

When I rise, Lady flaps her wings and I grab the handle of the pot.

"Oh, you don't have to," Scarlet starts when she sees that I mean to carry it back to their cabin for her. "I know you're already missing the party."

"Missing?" I ask, fixing her with a significant look and she smirks, for she knows there's only one reason I am going to Bram, the miller's. I understand the need for distractions and to that end, Megan is throwing a party for herself in her father's barn.

As we step away from the well, towards their home, I'm surprised to find Elias still standing outside of his library, watching us. His face is drawn and tight. So much so that I actually pause in my step to lock eyes with him in the scant light. My shoulders are square. My head high. Elias pretends to bat at a fly then pivots to head back inside. I resume my step before I draw much notice from Jasper and Scarlet.

Scarlet's fingers wrap around mine at her cabin door as she takes the pot from me.

"Thank you, Draven."

I incline my head at her smile. If Willow can calm the bee-letters in my chest then Scarlet can always remind them that they're strong.

Jasper darts inside.

She has to use two hands to hold the pot. She jerks her cowled head towards the main street. "Go. Dance. Laugh. Have fun. It's a good thing to have fun, you know."

With a wink, she steps inside after her brother.

I am left in the doorway with an expression I don't realize I'm wearing until it shifts. A smile.

As I walk away I laugh softly, even if just to try to expel the rosiness that's now warming my cheeks and neck. I reach for Lady and lightly dig my fingers into her feathers, rubbing at her soft skin at the base of the prickly shafts.

I watch the windows of the library as I pass. There is no sign of Elias.

Megan's family lives a short walk from the center of the village. Their home and mill is positioned beside a creek that turns the grinding wheel. There are plenty of candles lit inside the barn, making the windows glow brightly. Just as I'm thinking that it's frivolous to light so many instead of saving the supply her family has, I remember Scarlet's words and chase away the thought.

It's a good thing to have fun.

Someone's playing a fiddle inside. I can hear laughter and shouts. Dancing.

I know I shouldn't have brought Lady but I also know that if I didn't, I wouldn't have the courage to come, no matter how much I want to dance with Willow. After tying on Lady's hood to help shield her from whatever lights and sounds she will face inside, I enter.

The barn smells of fermented apples. Everyone has a cup of the golden liquid. Some have already had too much. Aiken seems to have forgotten that he can't drink as much now as he used to when he was larger. He is holding onto Megan's shoulders for support as he laughs. I'm surprised by the sight of her. The young woman's hair is twisted up with braids and pins in an elegant style that must have taken some time. She is wearing a dress so fine that I have never seen it before. Green skirts with a gold bodice. Maybe it's her mother's. Her grandmother's? Aiken's white tunic gapes and he hasn't bothered to lash it to him with a belt, or maybe his belt has been cast aside. He looks like a skinned squirrel still trying to wear its pelt next to her elegance.

A rush darts through me when I realize I didn't immediately spot Willow.

Where is she?

I scan the room. Megan's cousin, Felicity, who is only twelve, is playing the fiddle. Prudence is dancing with Geoffrey, a boy a few years older than me, her brown curls spinning out behind her as she twirls. Megan's mother sets out more ceramic mugs with hasty movements before ducking out the barn through the back, as if trying not to be seen.

But this isn't just a young person's party. There are people from the village who I didn't expect. A couple in their twenties. A woman who is at least Megan's mother's age is dancing alone. And there is Andrew who has always liked his drink, nursing a cup in the corner, wiping at his long white beard. Tension coils in my shoulders as I feel Lady's head swiveling around at all the input. I don't see Willow.

"Draven," Megan chirps. She slips away from Aiken and grabs her skirts as she darts over to me. "How good of you to come."

I nearly lean back when she plants a wet kiss on my cheek while resting her hands on my biceps.

She peers up at me with a smile, her breath smelling of stale alcohol. I part my lips but I can't even feel the bees because her hands are still on my arms.

"Well?" she asks with an expectant smile. Her red hair reflects the gold of the candlelight. "Aren't you going to wish me many happy returns?"

"I..."

Her brown eyes feel like they're trying to pull something out of me. Her touch is so light. I know my neck is leaning back but I can't seem to get it to go straight. This is worse than when she appeared when I was skinning the buck several years ago.

My jaw moves. I want to say it. To wish her a happy day of birth. But the bees are gone.

Megan's smile starts to dim. Her eyes stop trying to pull something out of me.

Aiken barks out in exaggerated laughter. She twists her head to peer at him.

The blacksmith's apprentice leans against the table, doubled over with mirth. As soon as he catches his breath, he lets out a fresh peal. The sounds make the bees of my letters begin to hum. I clench my jaw.

"Oh, stop it, Aiken," Megan admonishes as she releases me.

"I can't," he gasps. His eyes are watering.

The sight of his genuine amusement makes my skin burn. The bees buzz.

"You are horrible," she replies as she faces him, but there is something lacking in her tone. It isn't scolding.

"Where's..." I begin, so softly that I wince.

Megan peers at me over her shoulder with amusement in her features that sours my stomach. I clear my throat. "Where is Willow?"

"Aww," Aiken croons as he shoves himself off of the table and takes a staggering step towards me. "Isn't that adorable? He'll speak for *her*."

I know my face is growing red and I hate it. I want to walk away but my boots feel as if they are stuck in mud. I want to curse him but my bees are angry. I can't even feel Lady anymore.

"Of course he will," Megan mutters as she steps away from me and over to the cup she abandoned on the table, taking a sip. "He would do anything for her. Or is it Scarlet?" She arches a brow as she studies me over her drink.

"I know where Willow is," Aiken offers, standing up straight and willing steadiness into his voice. "Ask me, and I will tell you."

His cheeks are flushed with drink, making the brown of his sparse beard look like something that needs to be cleaned off of a dirty face. I look from his glassy eyes to Megan's, but she's pretending to be focused on picking at a thread on her bodice.

"Go ahead," Aiken encourages, taking a steadier step towards me.

It doesn't matter anymore that I'm taller than him. That I could best him in a struggle. That I hunt with the men and he doesn't. My mouth feels full of mud.

He shrugs his shoulders. "Ask."

I swallow. I order the bees to cease their buzzing. To calm. Only about half of them listen.

Aiken snorts then raises a hand to hide his amused mouth in a mock show of propriety.

"Go on."

I wince as I look away from him. Prudence is still dancing, though now it is with Aiken's little brother, Sven. Old Andrew tries to make his way to the barn door, holding onto the wall for support, his thin legs shaking. I can see Megan's mother in the ambient light outside, conversing with a friend.

"Oh, Draven," Aiken drawls. "Because I'm your friend, I'll tell you even though you didn't ask. Willow has already come and left."

He pauses, waiting for me to show some pang of sorrow, no doubt. Some pang of anything. I keep my head twisted away from him, still watching Andrew make his way towards the exit, his white beard sparkling with amber drops and shaking as he works his jaw.

"With Scott."

With Scott.

I'm peering back into Aiken's glassy eyes before I know what is

28

happening. They are siphoning off my every surprised breath as if I am somehow feeding his starving body. Making him taller.

Scott. He's twenty-two and known for his troubled vision. Back when trade was possible, he would often call on Willow's father, Cavan, to try out any new pair of spectacles he had acquired. Scott is tall, like me, only naturally much ganglier. He has a lovely voice and the girls in the village never seem to pay him much notice until he sings. Then they get all giggly. He must have been singing tonight. Willow has never so much as mentioned his name.

"They looked rather cozy in the corner," Aiken continues. "Talking until the cows come home." He snorts, undoubtedly realizing how inept his expression is these days. "Well, you know what I mean. Then they took their drinks and left. Almost touching he was walking so close."

"It's true," Megan affirms before taking another drink. "I never saw it before but I do now."

The bees are stinging me. No, it's worse than that. The heat is coming from the outside. It's coming from my skin. I'm burning and feel like a torch that everyone must see. Then I can't feel my feet. I don't even have a body. I'm just... just the burning. Inside and out. I can't look at anyone. I can't touch Lady. I can't move.

Willow wants someone else and I want her.

Aiken slaps my backside and I am snapped out of this heated trance.

Megan laughs. He shoves his mug in my hands.

I down the liquid without even tasting it. Without even noticing that my arm lifted it to my lips. The drink has an edge of vinegar because it's going bad but I like the way it burns differently inside than how I already am.

I remember Scarlet's words. "Go. Dance. Laugh. Have fun. It's good to have fun, you know."

I hold the mug back out to Aiken with a nod towards the barrel. He slowly smiles then claps me on the back, leading me to it.

Megan chuckles.

I drink another mugful. Then another. I let the burning of the alcohol spread to my fingertips and toes until it extinguishes the fire in my skin and breast that is from my knowing that Willow was talking with Scott. That she left with him. She could be kissing him.

The mugs all look the same. No, they're different. Some have a blue stain on the brown and some have a green. But I can't remember which color is mine. I just drink from them all.

I'm laughing. I'm stumbling. Aiken vomits just outside. Megan giggles as she swings my hands, trying to get me to dance. Are we dancing? I think we are. I'm dancing with Megan when I came here to dance with Willow. Megan's hands are soft. She steers me gently. Her eyes have a beautiful shape. They turn up at the corners, like she is always ready to laugh.

"You can bake," I say, surprising the both of us when we are swaying to an invisible tune. Her head is against my chest.

She peers up at me. Her red hair falls out of the elegant style. A braid now hangs behind her head like a tail. It's silky and reminds me of a fish. She is like a sleek salmon.

"You make mistakes but you can learn from them," I recite.

Megan slowly smiles. She shakes her head. "I don't make mistakes anymore."

I laugh because she sounds so confident, even if her speech is slurred. How ridiculous. How ludicrous. Everyone makes mistakes.

Mistakes... mistakes...

Through all the heat inside and the buzzing and the pain, like bites from a falcon beak in my heart, I know I have made a mistake. It was a mistake to place so much of me in someone else. A mistake to have expected anything. To have hoped. To have wanted.

Willow.

"Draven," Megan muses. "What kind of name is Draven? What does it mean?"

I find her eyes. They are tinged with the glassiness of drink and something else. A warmth I have scarcely seen directed at me. It's confusing on her face.

"Was it not you who sang by the well?" I softly ask.

A thin line forms between her brows and her step slows. We aren't really dancing anymore.

"He is a craven," I remind.

She loosens her arms around my shoulders the slightest bit. Her expression has grown terribly serious. Then she tries on a smile and lets her wrists rest on my shoulders. "They're words, Draven. Just words."

Just. Words.

In that moment, I am so full of envy that she can use "just" before "words" that I step away. She lets me go. Something has grown tight in my chest. It has to do with Willow and Megan and the fact that I brought Lady here. It has to do with the drink. It has to do with wishing every word wasn't such a struggle. It has to do with remembering a simple time when I would climb trees and marvel at their leaves. When I would listen, listen, listen for their voices.

Where did that boy go? He is lost in his own shadow.

Megan's mother collects her for bed. She offers me a blanket. I fall asleep on a pile of straw. Aiken snores somewhere nearby. We are left with one candle. In its dancing light, I see Lady perched on the rafter above me, her head tucked into her wing. It looks like there are two of her. Then there is another shape. A woman with brown hair and a long, white gown. She leans over me but my vision is so blurry that I cannot make out her face. Something about my Watcher is luminous. As if she can glow, and yet no light comes from her. Only from the candle.

The candle. Is it daylight or night?

When I realize it doesn't matter anymore, that nothing matters anymore, I laugh. The woman in white is gone. I fall asleep laughing.

Smoke. It burns my nose.

I sit up with a jerk. My head swims and I groan, struck with such a violent pain in my head and stomach that I'm almost sick. Lady chitters. This isn't my bed. I smell fermented apples and sweat. It's my own scent.

Blinking quickly to clear my eyes, I spot the lump of Aiken under a blanket a few yards away. Bram's barn. Mother will be wondering where I got off to. No, not wondering. Worrying. I rise and wince as the ground seems to shift beneath me. My hair is only half held back in its leather binding. My body feels foreign.

I will never drink again.

Smoke.

No, not just smoke. Stench. Something more than wood is burning.

Fitting. Fitting for the air to be so foul, for me to feel so awful now that I know what a fool I have been. My eyes burn with such sudden tears that I screw up my face to try to chase them away.

I reach for Lady and untie her hood. She flies a few laps about the barn, pausing on a rafter above Aiken. She poops. I almost laugh. My tears are gone.

Smoke.

I hold out my arm and Lady lands on it, the familiar prick of her talons comforting me. Together, we step out into the dim greyness that is both dawn and the brightest our sky will get today. Yawning, I shuffle towards the main street of the village, the creek babbling behind me, slowly turning the milling wheel. I can't go much faster than a shuffle without feeling as if my head will topple off my shoulders.

Lady chitters and I kiss her head. I still have her.

Someone screams. My veins are immediately thrumming. I'm running before I know why. They scream again.

Torture. Fire. Pain.

My head hurts so terribly as I run that it makes me fall. Lady takes off just before I hit the ground. I am sick. I vomit. More screams. Different voices. I shove myself out of the dirt and run again.

Once on the main street, I can see what looks like a large bonfire in the center of the village. A handful of people have stepped out of their homes. Husbands and wives are hugging each other as they watch. Only something is off. It isn't only pine burning. I can see black hair wafting upwards with the heat. A person. There is a person amongst the flames.

I run all the faster.

Then I see her. Willow. She's in her nightdress with her shawl around her shoulders. She is tearing towards the flames with a scream that doesn't sound like her voice. It sounds like every ounce of her being is rebelling against existence. She isn't slowing. She is going to charge into the flames. Her father is chasing after her but he'll never reach her in time.

I fly past the bonfire. Willow has almost reached the flames. I manage to slow myself just before our bodies collide. Her torso slams against mine and I wrap my arms around her to keep her from falling. She thrashes. Her screams make my ears ring and my head quake. She is fighting me. Escaping. I fight back. I wrestle her into the dirt.

Her father shouts at the pair of us. At Scarlet in the flames. I can't make any of it out. I do my best to pin Willow's arms to her side but she's much stronger than I ever thought. We struggle. I try to haul her away from the fire. As I do, I remember that there was a person in the fire.

Through the smoke and flames, I glimpse raven black hair amidst the bubbling, blackened skin.

It can't be. It's someone else. No, no, no, this is just part of the alcohol. A nightmare.

I drag Willow backwards. She collapses and I'm suddenly hauling dead, sobbing weight. I pull her to me. I try to cover her with myself. I don't understand how this could be. I don't understand what is happening. Shouts and weeping ring out around us. My eyes and nose are burning from the smoke. But all I do is hold Willow. I let her fall into me. She is so small. I wish my body could shield her from this. I wish my words could quiet her pain. But I'm crying, as well.

Scarlet is dead.

Wailing is in the air. Willow is trying to burrow into me and I let her.

My vision is blurry but over her head, through the heat shadows of the flames, I see Elias. He is watching me. He has the expression of a hunter who has just cut into a deer haunch at a feast. Something between anticipation and satisfaction. He holds my gaze until I have to turn away, my eyes burning.

# Chapter Four

**Eighteen**

---

It has been a year since Scarlet's death. I awake every morning to one thought: Willow is gone.

Scarlet died, taking half of her little sister with her. Even after I learned that Willow had left Megan's party with Scott because his dead grandmother had left a message with her for him, nothing felt the same between us.

The peace had fled. Willow was hurting. All the time. I could sit with her for hours, stroke her hair, hum "Midsummer's Song," and she may as well have been across the sea. When we were alone, it was no longer her and I. It was Willow and Draven and the smoke of that awful morning.

I let that distance numb my heart. I let it build a wall around how I felt. I let myself grow cold with her instead of blazing all the brighter for her. So that when she left, when she gave herself to him, I couldn't cross over my own wall to get to her. To ask her to stay.

Because there was smoke in our bond. Smoke between us. Neither could see the other clearly.

But what does that matter? What does any matter of heartache between two people who have shared so much matter? In the face of death, there is nothing more insignificant than wounded pride.

I should have stopped her. I should have told her how I feel.

Instead, I let her go. It was what she wanted.

I thought I was doing the right thing. Now I know there is no such thing as "right." All she did was a thing. A choice. An action.

She volunteered. On Midsummer, she sacrificed herself. As if being a Listener could somehow spare us all.

Willow is gone.

Every morning, I rise and head out to Sacrifice Rock. Every morning, I look for any sign of her trail.

*Look.* I don't so much look. Wasting a candle on my hunt would be foolish. I feel.

And every morning, I am disappointed.

Willow is gone and I let her leave.

When we eat our meager, watered down stews, my mother tells me not to fret. That Willow knew her own mind and had made her own decision. That it isn't my fault.

It is my fault. Everything is my fault.

Returning from the forest, I strip off my tunic and use the water in the basin to bathe off what little sweat I have shed in the cold morning. I hiss as the icy water leaves bumps all over my skin. I can feel my ribs like the details of a carved stone statue. Too near the surface. When my mother pushes aside the curtain separating her bed from the rest of the house, I yank my tunic over my head. I don't like her to see how thin I am. It worries her.

"I wish you would stop wasting such energy," she says flatly as she rises.

I secure my belt around my waist. "Good morning." Without looking at her, I grab my woolen cowl and head back out.

Small fires line the main street. There's no shortage of dead wood and the flames provide the only light. In it, I glimpse the shadows of

Morrot. I am a shadow of Morrot. I pass by the forge. Aiken was the first to die. The hammer is still sitting on the anvil, dusted by tiny ashes. I attended his funeral. Sometimes I stand by his gave. I leave pinecones instead of flowers. I don't know why. Maybe it has something to do with living so long in fear of him, but now he isn't living anymore so I have no fear of him.

I have no fear of anyone, in fact. Even death. I know it's coming for me.

Let it.

A door up ahead of me opens. A woman waits outside, bundled in a blanket. Elias is within, bowing as he accepts her offering of food. By tradition, each household in the village has taken turns feeding the village elder. I expected the custom to be rethought once food became so scarce, but no one was willing to make such a change. Elias claims that something upset the balance in our woods which caused the darkness. To upset any more balance could bring our deaths all the quicker. As a result, Elias has lost the least weight out of any of us.

I tug the hood of my dark green cowl over my head, wanting to hide my face from him. No, not to hide. I will never hide from that man. I just don't want to be seen is all. I don't want to feel his eyes hunting out my features like the ink on one of his parchments. Violating. His gaze feels violating.

I pass the well. I pass the place where Scarlet burned. I stride up to Willow's cabin and knock on the door. Her mother opens. She is still in her nightclothes, so I try not to look at her. Even though we have no means of telling time aside from the shape of the moon and the position of the stars when the sky is clear, decency is decency. She doesn't say anything, just tightens her shawl around her shoulders and shuffles inside.

Jasper peers at me from his place by the fire, wrapped in a blanket. I incline my head with a small smile and he rises, heading for me. His mother still doesn't speak even as I take the hand of her last surviving child and lead him out into the cold and the dark, shutting the door behind us. While still within the light from the cabin, I kneel and ensure that the iron pin and brooch clasping the blanket shut around the boy's shoulders is secure. I'm not really worried about it falling off, but it gives me an excuse to scoop him up. He hates being babied, but the fewer steps he takes, the more energy he will have.

Elias has instituted a curfew. We must not be seen.

Shifting Jasper to my back, we weave past the back yards of the houses and former shops lining the main street. The boy's thin arms wrap around my neck. Dead leaves and sticks crunch under my boots. Though I'm usually silent, it's more difficult even with Jasper's slight weight added to mine. I don't know if I will ever be whole again without his warmth against me.

Eventually we arrive at our destination, well, my destination. I don't really know why I keep bringing Jasper along with me other than because it gets him out of the house and is something to do. It's good for him to see that we are not *all* complacent. Or maybe it's more selfish than that. Maybe I just miss having a life at my side since Lady died. A companion. A friend.

Willow. Willow was my best friend.

I wrench her name out of my thoughts. I do that so often that it ought to be easier by now, but it isn't. Because when I let myself sit with the idea of never speaking to her again, my throat narrows and I can't breathe. And I must breathe. For Jasper. Megan. My mother. Willow's parents.

Bram's house would be impossible to spot if not for the dim light in the window. I use it as a point of navigation to slip into the barn. I let Jasper off my back. He stands still in the blackness, waiting for me to find the oil lamp resting on one of the rafters. Once I have it lit, I stride towards a stack of empty canvas flour sacks in the corner.

"They look like a potato," Jasper observes.

When I peer at him over my shoulder, there is a smile in his eyes.

I smirk. "I'll bet you could eat an entire potato that size."

He nods enthusiastically and I chuckle then set about shifting the sacks. He crouches in the ring of lamplight behind me, huddled under his blanket. Wood clanks against wood. I have found what I'm looking for. Crossbows, ten of them. While I'm no tradesman, I did my best to mimic the make and design of my own crossbow in their construction.

Jasper trots over once he hears, then parts the folds of his blanket. I hand him one weapon at a time, waiting as he tucks each in the pockets of fabric, securing them against his body. I do the same, attempting to hide the clunky items beneath my tunic and cowl. We are almost finished when there's the scuff of a shoe.

We both startle, but it's only Megan. She inches into the barn, peering first at me, then Jasper, picking at her dry lip. When she doesn't speak, I return to the task at hand. I don't need to ask why she is here. She has seen our light. After all, it's her barn.

Once we've clumsily hidden the weapons, I hold my arm out for Jasper and he presses his stomach to my back, gingerly at first, to avoid being pinched by the wood and metal.

"Why?" Megan asks as I wrap my arms around Jasper's legs. I rise. The wood clunks as it shifts.

When she doesn't inquire further, I pivot to face her. As a redhead, she was always pale. Now she is so white that even her freckles have nearly faded away. She stops picking her lip to study me, her brown eyes large in her gaunt face.

"Why move them at all?"

Jasper rests his chin on my shoulder. The weight of his head reminds me of my falcon.

"You know the risk," I say quietly. My voice is hoarse from not using it much at all today.

Megan's dull eyes travel to the empty flour sacks. Her voice is as listless as her arms dangling at her sides. "Is it such a terrible idea?"

My heart seems to perform two beats in the span of one. Because if Megan is turning, if Megan is swaying...

"We need to eat," she whispers, raising her brows at the brown canvas.

"Not like this," I reply, clearing my throat to force firmness into my voice. "Not with a lottery."

"We need to eat…" she repeats, still staring at the place where the weapons were hidden. "We need to eat."

Shifting my grip on Jasper, I step towards the exit, leaving Megan to her thoughts. We once again take the back route, weaving behind the yards of Morrot's main street houses. We are already out past curfew.

I don't like the dullness of Megan's eyes. I will need to rethink my strategy.

All the same, Jasper helps me stash the crossbows in my own barn.

As I carry Jasper to his home, my thoughts nearly sound like the buzzing of the bee-letters in my breast. Of course we need to eat. But I can't let Elias' lottery come to pass. I can't allow a friend or neighbor to be killed and divided up like cuts of beef. The thought sneers my lip and sours my stomach. The time for talking and planning and preparing is fast coming to a close.

I have spent the last few weeks pulling villagers aside, holding rushed, whispered conversations. Clasping forearms and making pacts to rise when the time comes. Promises of delivering weapons. But none of that will matter when that resistance is already being gnawed by the hope of putting something other than boiled dead leaves in a belly.

Jasper hugs my legs then heads back inside.

"Jasper?" I call as he's about to close the door. He peers at me and I offer him a smile. "I love you."

I have never said it before and he is so young. I don't expect him to say it back.

"I know," he replies, then closes the door.

My smile grows. It's starting to snow. As I walk back to my cabin, hidden under my cowl, I consider my options. I haven't yet had time to make bolts for the crossbows, which renders them useless. I haven't yet taught anyone how to use them. Haven't yet… haven't yet…

There is so much that I *haven't yet*.

In my barn, I light a rushlight. I set to work on the sapling branches I have been collecting every morning when I go out searching for Willow. Most wood has been dead for so long that it's brittle and spongy inside from the moisture always clinging to the air, but I have taken the care to cure these pieces. They are strong and straight.

I hope we won't actually ever need to fire them, but if we do, I want them to fly true.

Though I work for as long as I am able, I must sleep or I will be of no use to anyone. I retire to my bed.

The following morning, Elias makes an announcement. The lottery will be held tomorrow. The day has come. We have run out of time.

When I awaken, I do what I do every morning. Nothing ever changes.

Willow. I see her face. Her hollow, sea-green eyes.

As I rise and dress during what feels like the middle of the night, I try to talk myself out of the quicksand thought that I will never see her again. For I don't know that. All I know is that I will not see her again in this life.

I head into the forest, making for Sacrifice Rock. Only this time, I'm not looking for any sign of Willow. I am only looking for anything at all that might still be alive. A mole. A rat. A grub.

As I pass Sacrifice Rock, I trail my fingers over its frigid surface.

"I'm sorry," I whisper.

If she is watching me now from the Netherworld, I hope she understands why I can no longer search for her. To do so would be condemning Jasper to starve to death.

I haven't told my mother what I am doing. She frets every time I'm out breaking the curfew. As if we lived in town where neighbors could notice my slipping out. As if anyone would ever miss me at all.

There is a stream some distance away. I used to make a screen on the path to the water and sit and wait for deer. I don't know what could still be living out here, but I don't know where else to start.

It's cold out here in the darkness beneath a thin moon. Dew clings to the dead and dying branches. My tunic is soon moistened and I wish I had thought to bring my cowl. Though its heavy wool can weigh me down and make me feel clunky, it's warm and thick.

The tinkling sound of water reaches my ears as I near my destination. I pause, orienting myself in the darkness. I think my hearing has become even better these past few years. Or maybe I have just become more adept at relying on it rather than my eyes.

The crescent moon affords a faint, silvery light that filters in through the boughs. It would be useful were I in a clearing, but in the forest, it only casts confusing shadows that look like branches, making it more difficult to tell what is real and what is just the absence of light. Then again, what is real in the moon-shadowed woods? What is darkness and what is just the absence of light?

I know the stream is still thirty yards off. I'm on a game trail. The little section of rapids is about ten yards upstream. If I really focus, I can hear their...

*Snap.*

I hold my breath. Something else is out here.

My crossbow is in my hands and I am crouching as quickly as it takes me to pivot to face the direction of the noise. That was the breaking of a twig from a heavy footfall or a large body brushing past a branch. If it is not a man, then it must be...

*Crunch. Scuff.*

Was that a snort? I can't tell because my blood pumps so furiously that it's hard to hear beyond its rushing. I swallow hard and take a deep breath, trying to force calm into my veins. I will need all of my senses for what will come next.

This is a deer.

We are saved. I can bring home meat and marrow. Elias will have to postpone the lottery. No one will have to—

*Thump. Thump. Thump.*

My prey is bolting. In all my excitement I didn't even bother to notice if I was downwind or not.

I'm running before I know it. The sharpness of the dead boughs sting as I charge into them. I know I should be careful. I know that this is uneven ground and that I will soon reach river rock as I approach the stream, but I can't let this deer escape. Not when so much depends on it.

The animal crashes through the brush ahead of me, leaving a noisy trail. I follow. A part of my mind that still has space for laughter is amused by the fact that I'm now tracking sound rather than hoof prints. But that part of me is narrow and is soon squeezed out by the drumming need to kill and eat. My mother's lined, thin face is haunting my racing heartbeat, followed closely by the feel of Jasper's small weight on my back. The thought of them gives me speed I didn't think I still had.

I can't keep track of time, only of distance. I try to judge where I am based on the feel of the ground. I try to keep a sense of direction. I know Morrot is on my left, but that is all. If I get lost out here, then... I don't let myself finish the thought. I must remain focused on what is right in front of me.

Salvation.

# Chapter Five

I don't know how long I have run or how much sweat I have lost when I realize that I haven't heard a sound from the deer's flight for the length of several strides. I slow down but have to double over to keep from collapsing as I struggle to catch my breath. My arms are trembling and my lungs feel as if they have been dunked in ice from the frigid air. Snot runs from my nose. It's as if my body is screaming admonishments at me for having done something as foolish as run so much with so little energy left.

Though I try, it's some time before I manage to calm my heaving lungs enough to listen properly. I hold my breath for as long as I can.

Nothing. No twigs breaking. No mossy stones scraping. With a yowl, I rip off whatever is nearest me, a termite-infested pine bough, and hurl it into the darkness.

No meat. No marrow. No easy way to divert Elias from killing.

I want to rip off another bough but something catches the corner of my eye. I pivot to face it. There, several yards away from me, her form obscured by dead branches, is the gown of the woman in white. For the first time in my life, the sight of her startles me. She is so bright in the dark and damp. I can see enough of her face to make out her lips parting. Raising an arm, she points at me, her mouth suddenly agape as if to scream. It's enough to make me jolt.

Distraction.

A golden light suddenly blazes at my side. I instinctively turn my head towards it. A candle in a window. When I look back for my Watcher, she is gone. The candle, however, flickers like a question I am supposed to answer. I'm far from Morrot. There are no other villages in these mountains. The land is too harsh. So who lives here? In the dark?

Is it her?

After allowing myself a few more minutes to catch my breath, I start towards the light. My sweat dries, leaving a thin, chilly film on my skin. I wipe my nose with my sleeve. As I approach, the details of the window I'm focused on become bolder. It's glass with a painted trim. That alone is nearly enough to stop me in my tracks. It is a touch of refinement you wouldn't see at home.

This house belongs to outsiders. Outsiders who may have stores of food.

When I step onto the porch, the creak of the wood gives me pause. I hold still, my crossbow in my hand, ready to be raised if need be, my head bowed as I listen. The dancing line of the rim of the candlelight from the window wobbles back and forth. There are no voices. No one using the light that I can discern. This is good. It means these are people of enough means to burn spare candles for comfort. They surely must also have food.

Though I'm no longer certain of what time it is, the scant moonlight faded some while ago while I ran. It must be what would be dawn, or close to. Knocking would be rude. And my father used to tell me that homes on travel routes often have candles lit in windows to invite in passerby in need of lodging. These people must be generous. Kind.

I open the door just enough to unlatch it, then use the toe of my boot to swing it wide. The door bumps against the wall, louder than I anticipated. Or maybe it only sounds loud because the house is so oddly silent. Odd because it's like there is a blanket over everything.

The idea makes no sense and yet, even as I cautiously step inside, it's all I can feel. There is life in this house but something is dampening it.

A staircase lies directly in front of me. To my left is a parlor with two armchairs and a short table facing a hearth. Inside are dimly glowing embers. The inhabitants must be in bed, as I thought. To the right is what appears to be a kitchen, however it's too dark to say for cert—

Dark.

There's something about the darkness there that feels like I can touch it. I am as tempted to step into the blackness as I am to bolt. The hairs on my arms and back stiffen even more than they already have from the chill. I jerk my crossbow up, taking aim at nothing in front of me, and yet at something I'm sure is malevolent there.

I could have sworn I just heard a whisper. I feel as if a spider made of ice is inching up my arm, headed towards my spine.

A light. I hear a door open.

I pivot away from the kitchen, aiming my crossbow at the top of the stairs. There must be a lamp within for it's difficult to discern the two figures exiting in the brightness and I have to fight to keep my eyes from blinking. I aim all the same, though I couldn't hit anything in this blindness. The figures upstairs panic and shuffle.

"Draven!"

Whatever is blanketing this house closes in around me, for I'm no longer aware of where I am. I'm not in a parlor looking up the stairs. I am not hungry or frightened or cold. I can't feel the polished wood of my weapon in my hands. The only thing I know is the owner of that voice.

Willow.

I call out to her before I can even breathe enough to understand what's happening.

She was gone. Dead. Lost forever. And now she is here.

"Don't shoot!" she shouts as the person with her shoves her behind them, as if to protect her from me.

I'm climbing the stairs. The lamps on the walls burst to life and I nearly stumble but I catch myself because I need to reach her. But it's so bright.

"It's all right," she whispers in a rush but her words don't matter in this moment.

I shield my eyes at the top of the stairs and then it feels like she is everywhere around me. It's all I can do to wrap my arms around her in return. The brush of her curls. The warmth of her body. The hammering of her heart. She is real. Real and breathing. She smells of dust and cold and something else. Maybe someone else.

I have to look at her so I pull away. There are purpling marks on her neck. Bruises. I pull away to look at her, feeling the creases between my brows deepening.

"You're hurt."

The marks are yellowing on the edges. Healing. Healing because she was never lost, after all.

"You're alive," I continue.

Saying the word once doesn't feel like enough. My body is weightless as I'm pulled into her sea-green eyes. They welcome me the same way they did when I was just a boy.

"Alive?" I whisper.

She smiles and nods. There is a faint line on her forehead that tells me she never intended for me to think her dead. The lamplight glows softly on her pale skin and pools golden in her eyes, matching her hair. She is clean and smiling and the sight of her is enough to make the bees of my letters swirl and spin in a dance in my chest. I want to hug her again and not let go until the darkness has passed. I want to make her a crown of Lady's feathers. I want to build a fire so that she'll never feel chilled again.

My hand extends into the space between us. Her eyes move from my dirty fingers to my face. I only want to feel her hair. Soft as Lady's down feathers. Then everything in me smiles and she envelopes me again in her warmth. I hold her as snugly as I dare for fear I might hurt her if I squeeze as tightly as I want to. Her weight in my arms makes me feel weightless.

"What're you doing here?" she asks. "How's my family?"

"Hungry but alive," I reply, pulling away to look at her again, anxious to tell her how fine a person Jasper is.

"They think I'm dead?"

I nod but want to shake my head at the same time. It doesn't matter what any of us thought. All that matters is that Willow survived. More than survived. She is thriving. There is a glow about her, a lightness and ease with smiling that I haven't seen in her since before Scarlet died. As if she—

"Hello."

I incline my head and say my name in greeting without a thought. It's only after the words and actions are out that I remember that *two* figures exited the room. That the taller tried to shield Willow from me. Protect her. That the other is a man.

Given the way he is looking at me now, I have no idea how I over-looked him before. His dark eyes are sizing me up, sucking every part of me that went dancing about at the sight of Willow back into myself. I feel the stairs beneath my boots and the weight of the crossbow in my hand.

I take him in. This man is dignified and tidy. He has a fine white shirt beneath a black vest with a matching black pair of trousers. His hair is trimmed. Refined. I am suddenly tall with shoulders too wide and clothing too thin.

"Tristan," he says at length.

I look at Willow for some explanation. Instead, she tenses and presses her lips together, holding my gaze. Not now, her eyes speak.

"What're you doing here?" she asks again.

"You ought to have knocked," Tristan snips.

I stiffen because I know he is right. He would have every right to have me punished for coming in like this, if he wished, for clearly the candle wasn't intended as a beacon for wary travelers. Not with the welcome he is giving me. Willow seems to be absorbing his tension and Tristan relaxes, folding his hands in front of him. By means of apology, I hang my crossbow on my belt. It's the most I can muster at the moment.

"Following a deer," I reply.

48

"A deer?" Willow repeats, and the excitement in her voice tells me that this house doesn't have the stores of food that I had hoped. She is still hungry.

"Sounded like a deer. It led me here."

Now that my eyes have adjusted to the lamplight, I peer at my surroundings. The house has seen better days. The wallpaper is peeling, cobwebs are in the corners too high to be reached, and there is a faint scent of must and... iron. Blood?

"Do you live here?" I ask.

"Yes," Tristan replies, stepping up to Willow's side.

"How have you survived? Game this deep in died first."

"I didn't," is his answer.

His response reminds me of Aiken. He is teasing me. No matter. I am used to it. But he doesn't look amused and doesn't say anything further. Willow seems to have nothing else to say. The bees inside of me start to buzz heatedly. I have wasted too much time already.

All of Morrot is waiting. I will not suffer more niceties.

"If there is food to be had, then I must know," I begin, my voice firm.

I tell them about the lottery. That we only have until tomorrow before someone dies. Willow seems to shrink. The look of pain that crosses Tristan's refined face tells me that I was wrong to have thought he was like Aiken. That whatever his dislike of me, it's not because I am a shadow of a boy. It stems from something else.

Then suddenly, Willow's eyes are wide with alarm.

"You have to go," she gasps.

"What?"

Then they are conversing. Quickly. Quietly. It doesn't make any sense.

"It was her," Willow gasps to Tristan. "In the woods."

Who?

The panic in Willow's voice makes the bees begin to buzz in my chest and for a moment, I worry that they are causing me to not be able to understand what they're saying and why. But I don't need to understand why. Not when everything in Willow's body is trying to send me down the stairs and out of the house.

"Get out," Tristan hisses, taking a stalking step towards me.

But I can't leave. Not without her. I have to know she is safe. Jasper has to know she is safe. Her parents.

Tristan points to the door downstairs.

I reach out my hand for hers. Willow only stares. A cold I have never felt before pools in my empty stomach and frosts my chest. Her hand twitches but remains limp at her side.

"Willow?"

She shakes her head.

And that's all it takes. The frost spreads, creeping into my bones. She won't leave him. I don't know a thing about who he is to her, but she won't leave him. No, it isn't that. It's that she won't leave with *me*. I can't breathe. I can't breathe and the hive inside of me is spinning and thrumming.

Why do bees sting? Why do thoughts hurt?

Tristan is stiff, his brown eyes latched onto mine. He isn't as tall as me but I can read in his frame that he would tackle me down the stairs to make me leave if he had to.

And Willow... Willow is steadfast by his side. She is watching me as if worried that I would be the one to strike first. Me. As if I were like Aiken. As if I were some embarrassing remnant of Morrot that she had thought herself rid of. I can't breathe and the skin on my face burns. I can't hold my hand out for hers any longer.

"Go," Tristan commands.

I'm glad he does, for I can't seem to summon my own will anymore. I have none. For what use is free will when I am so unwanted?

Like a dead leaf, I spin and start clumsily down the stairs. After a few steps, I realize what I'm doing and rest my hand on the railing. I am walking away from her. I will likely never see Willow again. Peering over my shoulder, I look at her. Her pale skin and fair hair seem to shimmer in the lamplight. Her face is as familiar as my mother's, and yet, in this moment, as foreign as a stranger's. I realize that somehow over the years, she has become a part of me.

The Bee Whisperer. Willow. My friend.

But I am unwanted. She has asked me to go, and go I must.

I descend the stairs without another moment of hesitation. The frost in my chest is becoming suffocating. I can't breathe. It is so cold that it's hot. I find my own will again. I want to keep going. To run. To get as far away from her as possible. I need the forest and the quiet and a place to hide from this terrible suffocation that is my hive wailing in my chest.

Once on the wooden floor of the parlor, I'm tempted to run, but Tristan is watching. I can feel it. I will maintain whatever strand of dignity I have left. I won't run. I'll—

I hear Willow shriek my name at the same time that the black abyss of the kitchen surges towards me. I hit the ground hard enough for the air to be coughed from my lungs. Then all is blackness as Willow's cries and the sounds of breaking glass echo in the walls of my mind. There is pain in the back of my head. So much pain that I see lights that aren't really there.

Darkness envelops me and I welcome it. Darkness is an escape from my bleeding hole inside.

# Chapter Six

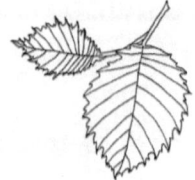

Humming. Someone is humming. Mother? No, that isn't her voice. She doesn't sing anymore. I can't recall the last time I heard anyone sing. No, I can. "Midsummer's Song" was sung by the village the morning we sent Willow off as a sacrifice.

There is a shuffle of bare heels on a wooden floor. The musty scent of damp furniture. This isn't my home.

I open my eyes to see a ceiling I don't recognize. Of course, the house in the woods. Willow. Tristan. They told me to leave. How did I end up on—

A low chuckle. No, a giggle. A woman.

Her dark shape is pacing back and forth in front of the candle illuminating the window. She is in a black, full-skirted dress made of far more fabric than you would ever see in Morrot. A long, black shroud falls down over the back of her head and shoulders, as if she has hair that goes on forever. She is smiling at me but I do not recognize her large, dark eyes or her heart-shaped face. She twists a string of pearls in her hands, sliding them between her fingers that aren't quite there.

Blinking, I tilt my head to try to clear my vision, but it isn't my eyes that are having trouble. The woman is enchanting. Her skin seems to darken with color just as swiftly as it fades away, like mist. I have never seen anything like her. I part my lips to ask who she is but the bees inside are completely silent. I have no letters.

Her color, along with her smile, intensifies the longer I study her. As if delighting in being looked upon. She bites her lower lip then kicks out the hem of her skirt with a short, high laugh.

"Well?" she asks. "What do you think?"

I am tired. I want to sleep. I want to go home. Stop Elias. But I don't even have the energy to lift my head off the ground. All I can do is close my eyes and swallow past the dryness in my throat.

Where is Willow?

"Oh, come now, don't be rude," the woman admonishes.

I'm startled back into myself by a stinging slap on my cheek. It rattles my eyes open and I realize she is leaning over me. I keep my face turned away all the same. As enchanting as her cloudiness is, I don't want to be enchanted by her. I don't want anything.

"I asked you a question."

I scrunch up my face, working my jaw to test the pain in my cheek. I have been hit enough times and have run into enough branches in the darkness to know when a bruise will form. She hasn't done much damage. Or so I thought. Her hand is suddenly squeezing my tender cheek as she grips my chin, forcing my face to turn towards her.

She leans in close, letting out a low exhale as she studies my face. I can't look away now. She is beautiful. Not in the same way that Willow is beautiful for her kindness or Scarlet was beautiful for her playfulness. This woman is beautiful for her confidence. Her selfishness. Her wanting. She desperately wants something. The gleam in her eyes is akin to that of hunger, but I know it's something more than food that she needs.

It is only after she studies me at length that I realize how her mist-like nature cannot be.

"Are you..." I try to ask, but my voice is so hoarse that I have to clear my throat.

She smiles as I do, her lips tight, as if she has some investment in my thoughts.

"Are you a sorceress?"

She arches a dark, thin brow. "Mayhap."

I swallow again, surprised that the words are coming so easily when I can't even hear or feel the bees of my letters at all. "A witch?"

Her soft chuckle sounds pleasant this time. Soothing. She is no longer gripping my chin, only resting her hand there. She has brown hair. She is luminous.

She cannot be and yet she is. Has everything in my life led to this moment?

"I am no witch," the woman quietly replies.

Her hand slides down my cheek to rest on my neck. The pulse of my vein there bumps against her cool skin. I ought to pull away. I ought to get up and leave. But it has been so long since anyone has looked at me like I mattered. Mother is too hungry. Megan only sees my surface. Jasper looks at me with need. No one sees me as something... significant.

"You have been watching me."

"How could I not?" she coos.

"What is your name?" I whisper.

She smiles again, running her thumb along the bottom of my jaw, over the stubble there.

"Victoria. This is my home." Lifting her gaze away from me for the first time, she peers at the peeling wallpaper and dingy rooms around her, sounding disenchanted as she sits up. "Well, it was once."

"Victoria..." I breathe.

Victoria closes her eyes at her name, as if savoring the sound. She rests a hand over the exposed portion of her left breast. "Too long," she squeaks. "Too long has it been since I..."

"Are you in pain?" I ask, stiffly propping myself up on my elbows, ignoring the dizziness of doing so.

"Always," she replies, bowing her head, her eyes still closed.

How did I get here, on the floor? How did I hit my head?

My crossbow is still on one hip, my hunting knife on the other.

Something came at me from the kitchen. I lean to the side to peer past Victoria at the darkness in the adjoining room but can't see much in the gloom.

Was it a man? An animal?

Victoria sniffles softly. "Then again, you know what it is like." She turns her head to face me, her dark lashes bedewed with tears that seem to shimmer against her misty skin. "You have loved her for years, haven't you?"

Everything in me tenses. I hear the first buzz of a bee in my chest.

"If anyone can understand my pain, Draven, it's you."

"How do you—"

"Willow."

My head aches with the thudding of my heart. It may be shaking my entire torso with each beat in my pathetic state but I don't care. Victoria seems to be able to see right through me anyway. She sniffles again but doesn't wipe at the tears shimmering in her eyes.

"I hear her talking," she explains with a small croak in her voice. She flits a hand towards the staircase. "To *him*."

"Tristan?"

"My *husband*," she corrects rather bitingly.

I'm sitting up all the way, ignoring the nausea in my belly and the pain in my head, for all I can feel is the twisting of the wound inside of me. Willow... and a married man?

"I know what you are thinking," she observes, watching me from the corners of her eyes. "How well did you ever know her, after all?" With a little shrug, she returns her attention to the pearls in her lap, rotating one in her fingers. "At least, that's what I wonder about him."

I shake my head. "No. No, she wouldn't—"

"She did," Victoria barks at me. "She already has! He was *my* husband." Her long fingernails prick at her chest. "*Mine*. And then that hussy appeared and seduced him just to spite me."

"To spite you? But she doesn't know you."

"She thinks I'm the Bringer of Darkness," Victoria croaks, giving me the most pathetic, plaintive expression.

"But you're just a woman."

"Oh, Draven, you sweet boy," she coos with a small, sad smile, her tears fading. "No one is *just* a woman."

There is something in the way she is looking at me now that makes me wonder where she was when I first arrived. When I met with Willow and Tristan on the stairwell. When I was attacked. For the first time I notice how cold it is.

Victoria sniffles and uses a portion of the veil hanging behind her to dab at her nose and eyes. "Look at me. What a mess. What a horrible, ugly mess."

"You are far from ugly," I reply before I even realize I am capable of the words.

She smiles at me, a hint of pink coloring her cheeks. "You really think so?"

"I've never..." I shake my head. "It is as if you... glow."

Victoria lets out a soft laugh. "I am glad you find my... condition so appealing. It is a family trait. Luminous skin in the darkness. It comes from being a... what did you call me? A sorceress?"

I sit up on my haunches, lowering my brows as I look her up and down more keenly. Never in all my life have I seen her likeness, except, possibly, in rare mushrooms that glow in the darkness. Then again, what do I know of the realm of the possible? Willow is a Listener. She can hear the dead. Why then should Victoria not have a touch of magic in her body? And what is solid in a world where Willow wants me far away from her, anyway?

"Tristan and I moved out here after we wed," Victoria continues, peering around the parlor once more. "To be together away from the crowds. You've never been to the cities, I can tell, but in the city, people like me are to be gawked at. Treated as some sort of... curiosity. Not a woman. Not a person. I'm very much like everyone else, only they choose to see me for my differences rather than my commonalities."

She bows her head, once again pondering her pearls in her hand. For the first time, I notice that large and small pearls are jumbled together in no particular pattern. As if the necklace were restrung after being broken.

"We found quiet here, Tristan and I. Even after the darkness began, we dared not leave for fear of what would happen once we returned to the crowds... I thought I had escaped their judgement forever, and then *she* came here."

Victoria fixes me with a wide-eyed, pleading stare.

"What happened?" I ask, even as I shift my focus upstairs, looking for any sign of Willow. I can only make out the dark outlines of the doors lining the hall.

"We invited her in," Victoria continues. "Fed her. Offered her shelter. Only to be repaid for my kindness by the girl accusing me of such horrible things."

I shake my head. The pain is lessening. Even so, I touch a hand to the back of skull, unsurprised to find some of my hair damp with blood. "She wouldn't. Not without—"

"Tristan."

When I return my attention to her, she offers me a small smile.

"Tristan was her reason. She wanted him from the moment she first laid eyes on him. She convinced him that my condition is the reason the darkness spread. That my skin glows because I'm absorbing the light or some such nonsense."

"Why would he believe her?"

"Because she ensnared him with her charms," she snips. "She is... young. Pretty." Victoria scowls. "Voluptuous." She runs a hand down over her own bosom.

The jealousy in her voice prickles my skin. I'm glad to still have my crossbow. I try to recall how many bolts I brought along.

"But mostly... because she is regular. Willow isn't like me at all." Victoria holds out an arm and slowly rotates it, watching the bare skin of her forearm ebb and flow. Her voice is just a murmur. "Sometimes the very thing that draws us to a person ends up being what drives us apart."

I want to argue with her. To defend my friend. To say that Willow is the last person who would ever do something to harm another. Yet Willow has harmed me, terribly. And ever since Scarlet died, there are parts of her that she has hidden from me. A hollowness and an anger at the world that I had thought to be a passing thing. Not a part of her. But they became a part of her.

"Yes," Victoria coos, scooting closer to me. "How well did you know her after all?"

The pain from the wound inside me is searing at the edges, climbing up my throat and making it tight. I couldn't answer her even if I wanted to. I can't meet her gaze. I can't meet her gaze because I can't hide the tears that I know are trying to burn into my eyes.

"How well do we ever really know anyone?" she whispers, so close that I can feel her breath. "We don't, Draven. Everyone keeps secrets. Everyone hides parts of themselves from the world because they are ashamed."

My jaw is starting to shake and I hate it because once that happens, I can never stop it. I know she can see the tears in my eyes as they blur my vision.

"Oh, darling," she coos. "Growing up is so hard."

Her hand is on my face again and I flinch as she uses her thumb to wipe off a tear.

"So very hard."

"I am already grown, thank you very much," I grind out between my teeth.

"In body," she continues, using her other hand to wipe away a tear on my other cheek.

I want to lean into her and run away at the same time. She is both welcoming and repulsive. Same and different. I let out a shaky breath. I have never had so much trouble with my own thoughts. Never been so confused. Because I am starving, exhausted, hurting, and Willow, my steadfast tree, isn't my friend.

Willow isn't my friend.

"There is so much more growing to do within, I'm afraid."

"I can't... I can't breathe," I choke out.

I don't know why I say it. I can breathe. I know I can. But there is something so tight and heavy in my chest that it feels like I will never breathe again now that I have to look differently upon every memory of Willow.

To have found and lost my Bee Whisperer all at once is too much. It's like traveling both up and down at the same time. My mind may as well be floating. I don't feel connected to my aching body.

"We are the same now, you and I," Victoria says.

Her hands are now supporting the weight of my head. I can't hold it up anymore.

"Draven." She turns my face towards hers until our brown eyes are latched. I can't see her clearly because of the tears but it doesn't seem important. I couldn't see her clearly before anyway. "Willow did this. Willow broke both of our hearts."

"Why?" I gasp.

"Lust," she whispers, wiping away another tear with her thumb. "After all, if we can never truly know a person, then we can never truly love a person. What else is there other than lust?"

After blinking several times, I can focus on her strange face. So eerie. So beautiful. So sad.

"We are but bodies, my dear boy. Bodies. We will all die. Most likely soon. Should we not use our bodies while we can? Should we not seek pleasure?"

My spine stiffens along with the muscles of my back. I sluggishly realize that my head is in her hands. That she is so very close. That I both welcome her words and want to send them far away from me.

"Tell me, Draven, did you ever kiss her?"

Leave. I need to leave this place. The cold in my skin is spreading gooseflesh all over.

"Did you ever kiss the girl you love?"

I squeeze my eyes shut, clearing the last of my tears. My jaw has stopped shaking. My breathing is calming. Her questions feel like they are on the other side of a frozen lake and I don't have the energy to cross.

Victoria's large eyes trace my features. A thin line forms between her brows as she runs her thumb along my chin, toying with my lower lip. No one has ever touched me like this before. I can't move.

"Darling, have you ever been kissed before?"

I can't shake my head. The effort would require me crossing the frozen lake and I... I know she can read the answer in my eyes anyhow. A little smile flits across her lips before she closes her eyes and leans in.

Her mouth presses against mine. Her kiss is cool. My lips are dry. I can't feel much of anything and all of this seems to be happening far away. To someone else.

She kisses me again, firmly holding my head in her hands, moistening my lips with her tongue. It is both warm and cool and tingling. I know I ought to kiss her back so I try to move my lips but it's awkward and I'm unsure if I'm the one doing it.

Victoria lets out a small whimper when she feels me return the kiss. Then everything is spiraling. Her hands are in my hair. On my neck. Her weight is on my lap, her knees on either side of my hips. She is pressing every inch of herself against me. I feel her hands and flesh as if through a layer of ice. She is across the frozen lake.

How do I cross it?

"Let's teach them a lesson," she pants against me between kisses.

Taking one of my hands, she places it on her backside. With gentle pressure on my shoulders, she bids me to lie down.

Across the lake, I see her smiling at me. That gleam is back in her eyes, like hunger, only not for food. She looks at me as if I matter.

Do I matter?

I'm lying on the ground now and my head aches from the press of the wood to my wound. Victoria starts kissing me again. Her weight is on my chest and hips. The ice between us is melting. I can feel her tongue and hands. The frozen lake is shrinking with every beat of my heart as one thought stirs the bees in my chest, over and over.

I do not want this.

"Are you watching?" she coos between kisses. "Does it hurt, darling?"

Watching? My Watcher has a Watcher?

"Yes," I whisper, though I know she isn't talking to me.

"Hush now. Hush." She slips her tongue in my mouth again but this time I shove it out with mine. She leans her head away with a small gasp.

I try to sit up but she shifts her weight to keep me down. I wait until her eyes have settled on mine before I speak.

"Stop."

Victoria flashes a brief smile. "Don't be silly. No man wants it to stop."

She cups my face with pinching hands, leaning down to press her lips to mine again. The frozen lake is gone. I can feel my body once more. Up is up and down is down and whether Willow is my friend or not, I do not want this.

"Get off of me," I command, and the firmness of my voice even surprises me.

Her lips go rigid against mine. She doesn't budge. She doesn't try to kiss me again, either. So I shove.

Victoria immediately counters, pressing her palms into my shoulders to keep me in place. I shove again and I am surprised by her strength as she wrestles with me. Then her lips are against mine again. She shoves her tongue into my mouth with a low chuckle. I can't push her out. I can hardly breathe.

What was it that came out of the darkness in the kitchen?

She grabs a fistful of my hair and yanks my head to the side. I yelp as the wound on the back of my head is pressed into the floor. Victoria drags her teeth along my lips and chin.

"You foolish, foolish boy," she growls as her mouth travels down my neck. Her tongue presses against the throbbing of my pulse beneath it. She traces circles with her tongue for a moment and while she is distracted, I thrash to try to get away.

Then I gag and yelp at the same time. Pain. Piercing pain. I freeze. She is biting my neck like a wolf or a cat killing its prey. My skin is being punctured. I can't move. All I can do is scream. She isn't just watching anymore. She is taking.

I don't remember the darkness returning. All I know is that I was in the parlor on the floor and now I'm outside. I can smell the sap of the dead and dying pines. Feel the cold flecks of snowflakes. Victoria is humming again and I am so cold. So very cold. Everything hurts. My neck throbs and aches with a pain so sharp that it's dull. Something is being dabbed against my wound.

For a moment, I hope that Willow has returned and is tending to my injury. Wiping up the blood. But the humming is too close to my ears to be hers. It is Victoria. I want to ask what she is doing but I can't find the heat inside to awaken my bees.

"There we are," Victoria chirps, pulling away from me.

I feel as if I am floating. My wrists are suspended above my head, held in place by something cold. When I try to move them, I hear metal rattle. Chains. I'm lashed to a stone. I crack my eyes open. In the dimness I can see the black of Victoria's figure. She is twirling a dead rose that she has coated in my blood. Closing her eyes, she takes a deep breath of its scent. Iron.

"So alive," she whispers on an exhale, the shifting colors of her paleness seeming to glow in the darkness of the outside world. "So alive..."

The sight of her strangeness and the memory of her bite help me feel my limbs again. I strain, trying to twist my arms free, but only succeed in rattling the chains. Victoria ignores me, her eyes still shut, savoring the scent of my blood on her bloom.

I twist. I groan. I yank and yelp. If anything, the chains somehow get tighter.

With a snarl I give up my struggle for the moment, struggling to catch my breath. Heat is sliding down my collarbone. I've made myself bleed again. Dizziness consumes me so suddenly that I worry this is all a dream. That I never really found a house in the woods where Willow was hiding. That Willow is dead after all.

What is darkness and what is just the absence of light?

I feel as if I have once again drunk too much cider and am spinning with Megan in her barn. Everything is muffled. The only sound is my pulse.

# Chapter Seven

When my vision returns, my chin is resting on my chest. I only realize that I succumbed to the darkness again when I notice that there is more snow on the ground. A proper dusting. Time. Time has passed.

And Victoria... Victoria can't be seen.

I shift. Everything in me is so stiff. So cold. It's so much easier to just lean against the stone behind my back and welcome the ice on its surface. After all, the cold numbs the pain. Perhaps this is what dying feels like. Giving in to the ice. I can do that. I can close my eyes and sink into the winter surrounding every corner of my being.

I can... I can...

My eyes are shut. I only know this because a match is suddenly lit by my face which startles me into opening them. The glow is brilliant and the scant heat from the flame makes me remember Lady's weight on my arm. Jasper's pale eyes. My mother's drawn face.

Life.

On the other side of the dancing yellow and orange are Victoria's shifting shades of skin. She is peering at me with such kindness. Such affection. As if she were tucking me in at night. I want to kick at her.

To bark at her to back away. To hit her. But I can't seem to move at all. It's as if my body is now one with the cold rock.

"Draven," she coos. "Draven."

Her hand is light as she strokes one of my cheeks. There is no warmth in her touch. Why is she so cold?

"Where is Willow, Draven?"

Willow?

In the cold. In the frost that slows my every thought and breath. She is in the darkness, that is where Willow is.

"She has not come for you," Victoria continues.

I can't do anything but watch her beguiling face in the flickering light. Revel in the small amount of heat. Cling to every word as an anchor to this world.

"You were only ever her shadow, Draven." She smiles as if she adores me, but the match reflected in her dark eyes illuminates a gaping hollowness that she can never fully hide. "You were only ever her shadow."

The light flickers. Her eyes drift to the flame as it sputters, her hand dropping from my face. Then it dies.

Her shadow. I have been Willow's shadow this whole time.

Shadows don't move of their own accord. Attached to their owner at their feet, they can only mimic, never lead. Never disobey. A shadow is a patch of darkness because no matter how good we are, we all do something to block the light.

I can feel body heat from someone so close that they're almost touching me. Then they are touching me. A hot hand on the ice of my cheek.

Shadows don't really have bodies. How can shadows feel?

I open my eyes. She is shining like the sun. I lift my head to look into her gaze.

Willow.

She has come for me.

I want to say her name. I want to reach for her but I am only cold darkness and shadows have no will of their own.

"Draven..."

My name is a dirge on her lips. My dirge. She will be the last thing I see when I leave this world. I don't mind. Because her sea-green eyes are filled with such fretting. Such adoration. Such love. Because there are more kinds of love than there are wildflowers, and each is just as vibrant and unique.

Victoria's voice comes from behind me, taunting Willow. They speak, but I don't care what they are saying. I don't care because love is light, and I can feel it stirring in me. Heating my veins. I love my mother and I love Jasper and I love Willow. I love the forest and the clouds and the storms. I love the bats and the molehills and the leaks in my roof.

I love being alive.

"I owe you such thanks," Victoria is saying to Willow. "I'd give it to you if you weren't a little whore."

I shift a shoulder just to see if I still can use it. It moves and sends my pulse throbbing. The wound in my neck aches but I welcome the pain, for pain means life. I twitch my other arm then squirm, worming warmth back into my limbs. Sorceress or not, I will not let Victoria be the reason I die. I will not be murdered.

So I thrash and tug. Yank and pull. The frigid chains don't slacken around my wrists but I'm growing stronger the more I struggle. I can do this. I can fight.

Then Victoria is back, leering at me while Willow watches, her mother's wedding dress looking brown against the white of the snow.

"Not a bad looking boy," Victoria says. "A little skinny."

I'm about to call her horrid when she grabs a handful of my hair and yanks my head back. The cry that escapes doesn't even sound like me.

"Is he yours?" Victoria asks.

No, I want to shout. I am no one's. I am my own.

But my bee letters have abandoned me and my neck is hurting so much that I doubt they could have flown past the pain, anyway.

"No? Well then."

Victoria's weight is suddenly on my lap. She isn't nearly heavy enough. In fact, I can hardly feel her at all. There is something terribly vile about her very existence. Her grip on my hair is tight. Light or not, I'm gathering the strength to try to buck her off when she speaks again.

"Or will you?"

Victoria bites me once more. I can't stop the scream.

I have skinned more animals than I can count. I know what is happening to me. She has already punctured the layers of skin and is now chewing on tendons as she tries to get to my veins. Arteries. To spill my blood like a river, as if I were a rabbit.

A rabbit.

*You are the rabbit's child. The acorn and the thistle down...*

I scream all the louder because I am not a rabbit. I am not her game. I am no one's game.

Then her weight is gone. Willow has tackled her. Victoria disappears.

Disappears?

I am done with this madness.

Done, done, done.

Groaning, I kick my legs. I twist my shoulders. I will break the entire rock I'm chained to if I have to, for I will be free.

*Free.*

Willow's hands are on me as Victoria chuckles. My neck and side are warm from my own blood. As much as the wound pains me, I'm thankful for the heat.

Willow yanks on my chains, trying to loosen them. I twist my torso until I can't anymore. Not because I am weak, but because the chains are somehow growing tighter as Victoria drones on behind us.

"What truths?" Victoria asks. "What laws of the earth exist after death?"

Soon, I can't move at all. I now know what it feels like to be an animal in a snare, or in Lady's talons. It doesn't matter how strong you are. Once in the grip of a predator, resistance hastens death.

"The living surround themselves with barriers but what do you really know about your world?" Victoria continues.

I stop struggling. Victoria sidles up to Willow who has her eyes latched onto my face is if I hold some power to drown out the woman's voice. As if she is weighted by terrible guilt. Victoria casts her dark gaze upon me for brief span, reveling in my vulnerability, before lowering her chin to Willow's ear.

"Can you really trust anything?" Victoria whispers.

Willow's hands still on my chains. I want to reach mine out for hers but she somehow feels as if Victoria's words are pulling her out of my reach.

"That is why we must take what we can while we can," Victoria continues to Willow, resting a hand on her shoulder. "There's no point in giving back. Beauty is for the beholder."

Though I'm still, the chains continue to tighten. Something is wheezing. Not something. Me. I cannot breathe. And Willow has the most wretched look on her face. As if she is a flame that has been stomped out.

No, Willow. I let you grow cold once when I should have been brave enough to warm you. I will burn all the brighter for you now.

As she meets my gaze with her troubled eyes, something softens inside them. As if she is listening to a voice only she can hear. Suddenly, I am reminded of her home, once full of laughter and Scarlet's stories told around a blazing hearth.

I am not prey. I am a hunter. But my world is now growing quiet. I can only hear Willow's voice.

"I will not take," she gasps then takes my hand in hers. "I will gather. I will receive. And I will give. I will give so much."

The chains are suddenly tighter. I will soon burst. Searing fire. Ribs are cracking. All I have are a pair of sea-green eyes. Then they're gone as Willow rises to be level with Victoria.

"And you," she snarls. "Will go back to the Netherworld where you belong."

Our tormenter lets out an enraged shriek. She raises a hand to strike Willow.

A brilliant light sears through my eyelids.

Then I'm a child in the mud again. Hands are pulling me out and holding me close. I can feel the stays in her corset. Her hair brushing over my body as she gathers me up in her arms.

The tenderness of Scarlet surrounds me.

The world is soft. I'm safe. I can breathe.

Heaving in air, I reach up and cling to Scarlet's bodice. I feel like I'm floating so I know she must be holding me. Carrying me far away from Aiken and the mud. Far away...

She is so incredibly warm. Her skin smells of dust and sweat. I only notice that her chin is resting upon my head when I likewise feel her hair against one of my cheeks. She is holding me so tightly. Her warmth thaws me. I don't know how long I cling to her, but it is enough time for me to warm up to the point that I can once more sense the cold.

It's only when I start blinking that I realize my eyes were never really shut. I am enveloped in gold and white. Gold. Not black. Not Scarlet. Not Scarlet because I'm no longer that little boy. No longer a shadow, hopelessly attached.

My bees shake out their wings.

"Willow?" I hoarsely exhale.

It feels so good to speak. To command myself once more.

She is here. Holding me. Because no matter what has changed, Willow is still my friend.

Murdered. My father was murdered. By Elias.

I don't let myself fret over the direction I am going as I pick my way through the darkness of the forest. Something deep inside of me, something primitive tells me where home is and I must trust it. After all, I have nothing else left.

Murdered. Scarlet was murdered. By Elias.

Spells of dizziness keep threatening to topple me, but so far I have been able to fight through them. Willow packed and dressed my wound. I drank as much as I could, knowing I need to replace the blood I have lost. I'm not tired or hurting or cold. I'm just two legs walking, taking me away from the decrepit house in the woods.

Murdered. Victoria was murdered. By Elias.

I was nearly killed by a spirit. Kissed by the dead. Tortured by the Bringer of Darkness.

No, I don't feel hunger or pain or exhaustion or cold because I am beyond my borders. In one night, I have been shattered and remade. I don't know what I am yet, but I know that I am no longer attached to anything. I am my father's pain. I am Scarlet's burning. I am Victoria's victim. I am Willow's leavings.

Leave. It wasn't easy to leave her behind. Not knowing that Victoria, the Bringer of Darkness, is still lurking about in that musty house. But Willow has chosen her battle and I have chosen mine. Besides, I can't break my stride now. If I do, I may collapse and never rise again.

The crescent moon is at an angle, preparing to set. I don't have much time left. Once it's down, the lottery begins.

Elias. He needs one more murder.

I grin once I catch a whiff of woodsmoke. Morrot is near. Death is near. But not mine.

From a distance, the candles and lamps in the homes of our village seem to move of their own accord as they're blocked by trunks and boughs as I walk. Another wave of dizziness hits me and I no longer try to explain to myself how the lights can dance. I just accept that they're waltzing.

Home. I am near home. My mother will be wondering where I have been for so long. Or maybe she won't have noticed that I ever left. I know it was only a night, but it feels so much longer since I last saw her. She doesn't know that her husband was murdered.

If I stop now to speak with my mother, I won't ever go out again. The part of me that is a wounded animal knows this. I'm no longer moving of my own accord, anyway. I'm animated by instinct: pain and the wild thrumming of my heart, the same way a rabbit or a deer can evade a hunter even after being shot.

There was once a turkey on the outskirts of our wood that lived for over a year with an arrow through his torso. Imagining myself as that bird actually makes me chuckle as I approach the house. Silencing myself as soon as I can, I worry that I am being overtaken by madness but can't really find it in me to care. I just need to stave it off long enough to do what has to be done.

The door squeaks softly as I ease it open. The house is quiet. I'm not even sure if my mother is home. The embers in the fireplace are dully glowing. I reach inside, snaring my cowl off of the hook by the door then recoil my arm. After easing the door shut, I gently tug the dark green hood over my neck and shoulders. It will both keep me warm and hide my bandaged throat.

My thoughts feel like my bees. Confused and buzzing about with damaged wings. I do my best to calm them. To focus them. But I'm not two yards away from my house when I hear the echoing of a bell being struck.

*Dong.*

Its ominous bass seems to travel through the darkness like the black sensation of nausea souring a belly.

*Dong.*

The sound seeps into my skin, pooling in my core. I stand up as straight as possible.

*Dong.*

My hand is resting on my crossbow. I no longer feel pain. The bees are quiet, waiting for orders.

*Dong!*

The lottery is beginning. I am ready.

# Chapter Eight

S triding towards the main street, I'm reminded of the sensation of
floating on the surface of a lake. As if my body isn't my own but
I'm in command of it all the same. I don't mind the feeling at all. In
fact, it drives me to walk faster, despite the throb movement brings to
my pulse.

Villagers begin to emerge from their houses. None are quick to
answer the call. I can hear someone weeping in the first house I pass.
After being away for a day, I'm struck anew by the scents of the
village. Dust and mildew. Decay. I had grown immune. The more
doors open, the quicker I must strategize. I am a hunter. I had meant
to make the first move.

I alter my course. Now that I'm back in Morrot, now that the bell
has been struck, now that the time has come, I'm able to remain tall.
Force my feet not to drag. I don't know where I find the strength, but
I'm able to sharpen my senses. Maybe it's from the water Willow gave
me. Or maybe it's because for the first time in my life, I want to watch
another human being suffer terribly. Elias.

I duck off the main street and knock on Geralt's door. His sister,
Ethel, answers. Geralt is nearly two decades older than me and
unmarried. Ethel and her two children moved in with him after her

husband left her nearly ten years ago. Now I wonder if he really did abandon them, or if he was just another victim. Nothing seems like happenstance anymore.

Geralt and his sister are among those I know I can trust.

Ethel's light eyes immediately dart over me as her brows lower and I realize that, even under my hood, I must be in a pitiful state.

"There is blood on your—"

"Is Geralt also at home?"

Ethel presses her lips together, giving me a look as if she is threatening to tell my mother that I am unwell. Then she nods. Her brown hair, flecked with grey, is pulled back in a bun. "Were you successful? Was there any game?"

I pivot to peer at the village behind me as it grows noisier and brighter. Footsteps and torches and lanterns.

"Is it time?" she asks.

Turning back to face her, I start to nod then stop myself with a wince. It's all the confirmation she needs.

A corner of Ethel's lips twist up in a smile. "Shall I cast the stone?"

"It's time for ripples but do not cast it," I reply. Stepping away, I'm surprised by the certainty in my own voice. "*Throw it.* With all your might."

Ethel nods and immediately shuts the door. I hear her calling to Geralt as I leave the house behind.

It has begun.

Elias is standing in the center of the main street in a ring of torches. I can't fight the sneer from my face when I realize that it's almost exactly where he murdered Scarlet. I want him to burn at the stake. I want him to feel the same pain he caused her. Willow. Jasper. My family. It takes everything in me to keep my hunting knife sheathed and to walk at a slow and steady pace towards him with the rest of my somber neighbors.

Something is building in my chest. Something that I have never felt before. I like it.

Several heads away, I spot Willow's mother leading Jasper by the hand. Her husband isn't anywhere to be seen, which reassures me.

The ripples are spreading. I want to go to Jasper and offer him some comfort, but I have no way of being able to predict what will happen after we make our move, and don't want to place him in any unnecessary danger. His mother is watching me, though, with a tight expression. I give her the slightest nod and her eyes slide away from mine. I don't blame her for being cagey. She knows what's at stake.

*Dong. Dong. Dong!*

Standing on a stool, Elias hits the bell he is holding again, flapping his brown robed arms to encourage the villagers to step closer. I shuffle ahead with the rest. Every once in a while, I mistakenly turn my neck to try to see around my hood. Sweat beads on my brow from the pain I've caused myself. To ignore it, I focus on the sensation building in my chest. I feed it. It rumbles. It is not made of bee-letters.

"Good people!" Elias bellows, throwing out his arms.

He licks the spit off of his lower lip as he surveys the crowd. We've gathered around him on all sides, but no one seems to dare enter the ring of torchlight encircling him. In the yellowed, flickering glow, no line or crease is hidden on his face, yet I cannot see an aging man. I cannot see a person at all.

I am a hunter. I see only prey.

"We gather here today under the direst of circumstances yet faced in the annals of Morrot," Elias announces.

He lowers his arms. The fire reflects in his eyes as his lax face surveys the people watching him, as if he is filled with regret. Perhaps he is. A flame of compassion sparks to life in me but I only have to remember my father to stamp it out. Elias forfeited his right to compassion long ago when he made the choice to take human life.

A baby fusses. Several people are coughing. In the distance, I can hear the roar of the wind cutting through the dead and dying trees. Then footsteps scuff. A handful of people turn to look to see who has arrived. It's Geralt. I keep my expression calm as I once again pivot to spot Willow's mother. Cavan is back at her side and she is holding Jasper.

Good. The ripples are growing.

"Alas that we are being punished for trespasses still unknown to us," Elias continues. "Alas that all of our attempts to appease the Bringer of Darkness have failed. Alas that we now must resort—" He cuts himself off with a small choking sound, hanging his head.

A woman wails. It's then that I realize that most of the people coughing are actually crying. I scan the heads in front of me and spot Ethel's bun. One hand holds her cloak shut while the other grips something hidden beneath its folds. I almost smile but then I feel the pressure of someone watching me. A few people to the left of Ethel is a shock of thinning red hair.

Megan.

Her pale, gaunt face is turned towards me. Though her eyes are dull, they manage to tug on me all the same. For she is hoping that neither of our names are drawn. In that moment, I realize that I have been wearing blinders. Megan was only ever in my peripheral vision, even when she was standing right in front of me. My heart stutters at the thought. It almost kills the thing building in my chest, so I look away. For too long I couldn't look at anyone who wasn't Willow.

Elias is speaking once more with unshed tears in his eyes.

"Fate shall govern this choice. Whoever is chosen must go willingly. It is your solemn and final duty. Remember young Willow and her courage. She was unfaltering as we must be now."

Elias pulls a scroll out from his robes and slowly unfurls it. I'm tempted to shoot him now for the mere crime of mentioning her name. She is dead to him. How little he knows. How little he has ever known.

"Here is a registry of every household in Morrot." The parchment crinkles as it's unrolled. His voice is soft which prompts the crowd to quiet to listen. "The names on this list are all good people. Peaceful people. Families..." He pauses as he peers out at the crowd. "Families... Individuals who have nothing but my utmost and heartfelt respect. There is no greater pain than choosing one of your names."

My pulse feels thick. It is in my wound and my ears and my head. It is feeding the thing in my chest. I slowly unhook the crossbow from my belt. The inked names are illuminated in the torchlight through the back of the parchment, and in the quiet I wonder which word belongs to which villager. Quiet. Elias lowering his voice brought about quiet from the village. He still has more respect than anyone else in Morrot. I realize with a skipped heartbeat that I didn't think this through. Not properly.

I never intended to spend so much time in the woods yesterday. To be held prisoner in that fetid house. I wasted valuable time that I had been counting on using to form a plan for what is to come after today. Stolen moments and muttered words of comradery are only enough to light a spark. We are armed, yes, and those who are await my lead, but I see now the folly of having thought that weapons were enough.

At my signal, we will surround Elias and take him into custody. That may be enough to stop Elias from picking a name, but it will not usurp him. Even in chains, he is still our leader in many villagers' minds. I don't know how to control this fire once it's blazing.

I must expose him for who he really is. For what he has done. But it will be his word against mine. Unless...

A gasp and a wave of murmuring rises up from the crowd and I realize that I have been so focused on my own thoughts that I blocked out Elias' voice. He is gazing out at us with a sneer, surveying the faces.

"That is right. One of us is a traitor." The skin between his nose and upper lip trembles and the unshed tears in his eyes seem to quake. Or maybe they were never tears at all but just a trick of the torches. Irritation from smoke. "That traitor shall be the flesh we feed upon."

Cavan is gazing at me in alarm as people begin shouting, asking for names. For the first time, I notice that Bram is standing at Elias' side. Bram the miller whose barn I used to hide our crossbows. Megan's father.

Betrayal.

The thing growing in my chest surges and swells.

He knows. Elias knows.

Ethel is peering at me over her shoulder, her light eyes large. She subtly jerks her crossbow in silent question. I give her the slightest shake of my head. We no longer have surprise on our side. We need a new plan.

This is the moment when the buck has caught our scent and is crashing through the trees. A hunter has to decide if it is best to fire a non-lethal shot and wound the deer to slow it down, or to let it go. Those who don't have to collect their own food often don't know that the meat can go bad even while the prey is alive. A wounded animal that has had the time to flee before death will have fetid meat. Likewise, if I injure or kill Elias now, I will spoil everything. I will—

"Draven Lucian's Son!"

The sensation of floating that I have been trying to keep at bay comes surging back. I know it's from losing so much blood and using my body anyway, but something else about this moment feels like a dream. People are looking around, trying to find me but my cowl is up. I know I am breathing but I can't move. As if I'm watching this all happen to someone else rather than playing a part. Adrift.

Then someone behind me yanks my hood off. My mother wails as I am revealed.

"Seize him," Elias shouts. He points at me with his long, shaking finger, a chipped, yellowed nail curling at the tip.

Hands are suddenly on my biceps. Amidst the shouts of anger, there are several asking for this to stop. To let me go.

If I could speak, I wonder what I would be saying.

Elias curls his finger in towards his body, his eyes locked onto me. He was never the prey at all. I was. I'm the wounded buck only I didn't have the instincts to catch the hunter's scent. To run. To survive. The men holding me walk me forwards. I step lightly and weightlessly along with them. The crowd parts to allow us to pass. All except for Ethel. She hesitates, once again meeting my gaze. I shake my head the slightest bit.

Not yet. Not yet because I can't tell if I am a buck or a boy. A shadow or a body.

Think. I have to think.

What am I?

The thing in my chest rumbles.

"Silence!" Elias is shouting at the crowd. "Silence!"

I'm wrenched to stand beside Elias on his stool. He towers above me. Someone is restraining my mother. Ethel has made her way to her brother and they are speaking animatedly. Ripples begetting ripples. Megan is in tears and screaming at her father who is pretending to ignore her but his jaw joints are quaking.

Think. I have to think.

Who am I?

The thing in my chest sends a tremor through my whole body.

"How many of our children will you take?" Cavan bellows, his voice rising above the rest. That quiets the village more than Elias' demands managed. The words around me bounce off of my head, trying to get in. To anchor my adrift mind.

"This man is no longer a child," Elias replies, jerking his head towards me as he rolls up the scroll.

"He is my *son*," I can hear my mother shouting. "My son!"

The desperation tearing at the edges of her voice makes everything start to go quiet.

Think. I have to think.

Am I a shadow or a boy?

The thing in my chest goes quiet as it coils.

The grips on my biceps grow painful. Painful because my knees are getting weaker and these men are suddenly supporting more of my weight. I start to wonder who they are but no longer feel like I'm floating. Instead, I am slipping under water. I'm drowning.

No. Not now. Not yet.

I am a thinking thing.

I kick for the surface of my mind.

I am not a shadow or a boy.

Blinking, I give my head a shake and lock my knees.

Elias is speaking to the crowd once more, the long fingernail of a hand pointed at me. "...Conspired. Plotted. He would have you all be leaderless until every last one of you is dead. For his crimes, he shall be the first selected."

My mother is still crying. I hold my head high. Each gasp she utters twists the coiled thing in my chest and for the first time since I set out into the woods yesterday, I can again feel the gravel beneath my boots. I am awake. Awake and ready to hunt.

I will not be prey, but I haven't concealed my scent. A startled boar or stag will charge. Many a good hunter has been gored, but not me. Not until now. Am I fast enough to make a killing shot?

Elias looks down upon me from either side of his long nose. Were I more fully in myself, I would be disgusted by the excitement in his eyes. I would struggle and glare. I have only ever been the boy smashed in the mud to him. Willow and Scarlet's shadow. The one who has seen all of his lusty looks.

My tender wrists are scratched. Someone is binding them behind my back with twine. They are already bruised from Victoria's chains and I welcome this new sting. It sharpens my senses. Pain is life.

Withdrawing a knife from his robes, Elias makes a dramatic show of holding the weapon up high. It is enough to silence all but the very young who only know the gnawing of their aching bellies. That knife is for me. In the torchlight, it looks more orange than silver. Like something otherworldly.

Elias pivots to face me. His nostrils flare with each noisy breath. He is savoring this moment the same way he savored staring at Scarlet and Willow.

"You made a mistake, boy," he lowly drawls. "And now, I will gut you for it."

I know Ethel and Geralt and the others are confused. That they are awaiting my order. An order I cannot give if I'm dead. But though the prey is fleeing and I'm gored, I may still have the element of surprise. I am a thinking thing, and I now know what has been growing and coiling in my chest.

Elias cocks his head, studying my neck. As far as I know, he has never killed with his own hands. I'm not the only one who didn't completely plan everything through. He is wondering how to go about it.

He jerks his head to the men behind me. "Remove his cowl."

I hiss in pain as they do so, yanking the coarse wool over my wound and my hair. Though I feel a rush of fresh air in the absence of the garment, I don't feel the rush of cold as I ought to.

Elias' eyes narrow as he studies my neck and I feel the warmth of satisfaction as several onlookers notice, as well. I can feel a dozen questions in the gazes around me. My wound is my weapon. My only proof.

"Have you some disease?" Elias hisses, leaning back the slightest bit. "Some ailment?"

My bee-letters are gone but I know he can read the challenge in my eyes as I keep them fixed on his, unblinking. Elias licks his lips, his gaze lingering on my bloodied bandages. He is struggling, fighting to put the pieces together but he doesn't even know what the pieces are. He doesn't know that *I* know.

"How came you by this?" He gestures to my bandages with his knife.

Unbidden, a smile slowly spreads across my face. Elias' pale eyes dart about my features, desperate for some clue. Some tell as to why I am not trembling at his feet. Then his gaze stills and his sneer relaxes.

He knows that I know. The hand holding the knife shakes.

"I was attacked," I reply, low and slow. "By the Bringer of Darkness."

Elias' features slowly recoil, making him look twisted and confusing, like a knot in a piece of wood. The murmurs and shouted questions of the people around me are a boon to my strength. The gravel beneath my boots is packed firm. I'm on solid ground. Though I sway the slightest bit from each heartbeat, I am not shaking. I'm as strong as the resolve that has grown in my chest.

"Willow saved me."

The shock that reverberates in the air around me laps at my ears like invisible waves. Yes, Willow saved me. Because Willow is my friend and I am hers and I am standing on my own two feet.

Elias darts his head, assessing the reactions of the crowd. Willow's family is silent. I don't look for them. Instead, I let my eyes drift to the gravel. There, in the dancing torchlight, is something I haven't noticed in a long, long time.

A shadow. My shadow.

I have a shadow, too, because I'm solid and strong and I love my mother and Jasper and Willow and mostly because I love whoever I have yet to meet. I love tomorrow.

The thing in my chest is coiled so tightly now that I know it's just waiting for me to release it.

"Willow?" Elias snarls. I can only see the darkness he is casting upon the ground as he leans towards me. "Willow is dead."

That's all it takes. I do something I have never done before in my life. I spring the coil in my chest. It is the cold thickness of the mud in my mouth as a child. It is the taunting of Aiken at Megan's party. It is years of giggles and whispers and stares. It is a shout.

"No, *Scarlet* is dead," I bellow, lifting my head to look him in the eye.

Elias blinks in surprise, lowering the knife as he flinches from my outburst. I know I should be measured. Thoughtful. But something has broken in me and I can't contain it now. These aren't the bees that I have struggled with my whole life. This is a torrent.

"Scarlet is dead because you killed her when she discovered that you had murdered my father! You killed her because she would not lie with you. Because she would never care for you. You killed her because Scarlet was kindness and love and courage. Scarlet was clever and joy and a gift to the world."

Elias shouts, trying to be heard over me. The only word I can make out is "lies." He gestures wildly to the men holding me then hops off of the stool, pointing at the seat. As if it were a butcher's block.

"You are filth," I snarl, even as the men shove me towards the stool. "*Filth.*"

"Kill him now," Elias screeches, the whites of his eyes far wider than I have ever seen. "Death to the traitor!"

There is such uproar around us that I can't make out any of it. All

I know is that bodies are shifting and moving and I can't stop shouting.

"You killed my father because he knew about the house – that there is a world so much grander than our valley!"

"Silence," Elias crows.

The men behind me kick my knees. I drop to the dirt like a sack of flour. They wrench my shoulders towards the stool but still I cannot quiet.

"There is a house in the woods," I continue. "Willow is there now, battling the Bringer."

The men try to force my head onto the stool seat but I twist and fight. They shove my shoulders backwards instead. I cry out as the back of my skull hits the wood. Nothing about this is natural.

For the first time, I realize the villagers are fighting. Some are trying to get to me and it isn't just the Ethel, Geralt, and the others. I see Megan and the blacksmith and even Andrew, the old drunkard, waving his withered arms. They are kept from me by those loyal enough or hungry enough to want to believe that I am lying.

"Willow is alive," I scream out past the pain in my neck. Out of the corner of my eye, I see the orange flash of Elias' knife. "She is alive!"

I can hear her mother screaming questions, wanting to know how to get to her daughter.

People are shouting. The scuffles have escalated into brawls. Neighbors are falling. Bleeding. One of the men who is holding me down shouts at Elias to kill me now.

In my twisted position, I can only see the darkness of the sky and the dancing tips of the torch flames in a circle around me. Their smoke that seems to disappear into the night. Then Elias' face looms over me, the knife trembling in his hand. He licks his lips, surveying the sweat beading my hairline. One of his fingers drifts out and drags across my skin, wiping up some of the moisture. He rubs it between his thumb and forefinger then closes his eyes and inhales the scent. The sounds of the fights are quieting. No one has the strength to resist for very long.

"Now," one of the men restraining me hisses. "Kill him now."

I finally recognize his voice. It's Scott, the singer always in need of spectacles. Though I don't know how, my heart dips a little.

Elias opens his eyes, studying my face as if the scent of my sweat wasn't satisfactory. Then he raises his eyes to Scott's and I realize why. Killing me now is akin to admitting his guilt.

"What," Elias drawls loudly, "possesses you to say such false-hoods, Draven Who Does Not Speak?"

I clench my jaw for a moment before replying. "The truth will not die with me. Willow knows. Now everyone knows."

"Queer, is it not, that Draven Who Does Not Speak has suddenly taken to bellowing?"

One of Scott's hands grows lax and I try to jerk my shoulder free, only to have him hold me down all the harder. I wince, hissing because everything hurts.

"Even his own mother must be shocked by this... outburst," Elias continues to the calming crowd. I can only see his face from below but he pauses to eye the knife, turning it over to play with the reflecting light surrounding us. "Gwen, have you ever known your boy to raise his voice?"

While I cannot see my mother, there is tension that I know means heads turned towards her, awaiting her reply. Her lack of one is answer enough.

"So I thought," Elias continues, and then swings the knife to gesture to me. "This is not your boy, Gwen. Some evil spirit speaks through him. Draven is possessed by the same dark magic that corrupted that witch, Scarlet!"

# Chapter Nine

Cavan is the first bellow I hear trying to shout Elias down, but even more seem to cawing in agreement with our village elder. I close my eyes.

Think. I must think. I am a thinking thing.

"Willow is dead. We sent her as a sacrifice. Now this madman would have you believe that she is alive and that I am somehow responsible for his father's death? We all know that Lucian fell while hunting."

Several murmur in agreement, but even more terrifying is the relative silence as Elias builds his case against me. After all, who am I to them? The boy with the falcon. The one who hunts with the men because quietness is a hunter's gift, but a man's curse. I was born with mud in my mouth. I am Draven Who Does Not Speak. I am the rabbit's child. The acorn and the thistle down. Why should they pay me any heed at all?

Think. I must think.

"The poor man hit his head. And now this demon boy would have you believe that I..."

Demon? Think!

I can't hear Elias anymore.

I don't know if my bee-letters will ever return.

Think!

I see Scarlet's blazing blue eyes. Hear her laugh. Smell the fetid burning of her raven dark hair.

"...After all of the sacrifices I have made for Morrot," Elias is hissing. A drop of his spit lands on my lips. That's when it comes to me. It stokes the tightness in my chest. "Scarlet was my greatest pupil. Never in a thousand years would I wish that girl harm. She—"

"Library," I bellow, silencing him.

I open my eyes. In the distance, all I can hear is the wind cutting through the trees and my own panting.

"It is in the library."

"What," Elias snarls, leaning over me, the skin between his nose and upper lip taut like a bowstring, "is in the library?"

I lock eyes with him, gasping past the pain burning in every joint and muscle. "My father's necklace. The one I made for him out of Lady's feathers. It's in the library where Scarlet found it before you murdered her."

A white sheen seems to pass over Elias' features, like the film that crosses over an animal's eyes the moment death takes its body. He is paralyzed. Paralyzed because only Scarlet knew about my father's necklace. Scarlet who took that knowledge to her grave.

He doesn't know Willow's secret. No one does. Elias doesn't even take a breath.

"Now," I scream.

There are shouts. Cries. A whir and a thud and suddenly Scott's hands are no longer holding me down. He has been hit by a crossbow bolt. The other man releases me, as well, and I topple over. Relief floods my joints and flesh as I hit the dirt like a ragdoll, blood returning to contorted limbs. The dimming of the pain is so pleasant that I close my eyes. I could sleep here.

It's oddly quiet as feet shuffle around me, scuffing in the gravel. Elias is groaning, weakly resisting as he is surrounded. Then a strong grip is on my bicep, hoisting me back upright. The motion makes my head spin and wakes me from some of my sleepiness. For a few moments nothing is in focus, and even when it is, it's difficult to make out his features now that I'm in the shadows of the villagers surrounding me. I eventually realize that it was Cavan who helped me up. Then my mother is on her knees beside me, holding my face in her hands and asking me to look at her.

Why is she asking me to look at her?

Blinking, I realize the world had grown muffled again and I hadn't even noticed it happening. That I was so relaxed because I felt like I was floating. I focus on the pinch of the gravel against my kneecaps.

"Mother," I whisper.

Though she smiles, there are tears in her eyes. Her hands feel so warm against my skin. I'm so cold.

Elias has been overpowered. I don't need to twist my head behind me to see that much. I can tell by the arguments alone. Some are calling me a liar. A demon. Someone takes a kick at me but is shoved away by Cavan before the blow can land properly. It merely glances my hip and I can't find it in me to get angry. Scott is on the ground moaning. Others are asking my mother if what I've said is true but she is ignoring them.

Willow's father pulls out a small knife and reaches behind me to cut my hands free, only to be stopped by the blacksmith.

"We don't know anything yet," the once burly man cautions.

Cavan looks from him to me, his blue eyes blazing with frustration for the span of several heartbeats before he nods. He raises his voice to a shout. "Very well. To the library!"

With that, he hoists me to my feet. My mother is shoved out of the way, replaced by the blacksmith as they help guide me along with the crowd towards the building.

At first, it's all I can do to focus placing one foot forward, and then the other. Eventually, I lift my heavy head enough to peer about. For a moment, everything twists and blurs together. Then my pulse calms. Villagers grabbed the torches and are bearing them to light the way.

Ethel and Geralt and two others that I armed are escorting Elias at crossbow point. He shuffles along in their midst, fixing me with an expression somewhere between a glare and a frightened apology. As if I have the power to save him. I suppose in his mind, I do. After all, I have the secrets of a dead girl in my head now and he doesn't understand how they got there.

The brush of a beard against my cheek distracts me from Elias. Cavan is speaking lowly in my ear as we slow to a stop outside of the building.

"You saw her?" he breathes. "You saw my daughter?"

There is a rasp to his voice that I have never before heard. Like chapped hands clinging to an icy ledge. Desperation.

We are all desperate.

I turn to look him in the eye. Our faces are only inches apart. His bloodshot gaze searches mine and I will every image I have of Willow in the house to him, because my bee-letters are gone and the shout in my chest has been spent.

A line forms between his dark brows, creasing his pale skin. I have had my ears boxed by the butcher for such silence. Been chased by the son of a traveling horse tack salesman. Slapped by the woman spinning yarn for my mother. All because they asked me questions when the bee-letters were gone. But Cavan... Cavan once taught me signs with my hands to use while hunting.

I can feel the burning of his question in his very pores but he doesn't badger me. His eyes leave mine, trailing down to my neck. He is holding my bicep with one hand but uses the other to brush his calloused fingertips across the edge of the linen bandages on my throat. The moment he does so, a softness settles on his features, as if he can recognize the work of his daughter's hands. When his gaze returns to mine, he appears both younger and older. He sucks in a small breath, as if to thank me, when there is a thud.

The library door has been kicked open. People rush in.

The blacksmith marches me forward so Cavan complies. I only vaguely notice someone stepping on my toes in their boots as villagers' bony bodies shove past each other to get inside.

I admire the interior of the building, for I have never been within its walls. There are scrolls and leather-bound books lining the shelves. Inside, I know there are printed shapes that are the same as

86

my bee-letters, only a person doesn't have to have a voice to under-stand them. Only a mind and eyes. In a different life, perhaps Scarlet could have taught me to read, as well.

"Where?" a villager shouts as people begin pulling the tomes from their shelves. "Where is it?"

"Folly," Elias shouts from nearby. Ethel and Geralt have their weapons trained on him only a few yards away from me. "This is pure folly. I have no such talisman from Lucian or any other."

The noise in the room grows and the thudding of falling books seems to quicken my pulse. I can feel it throbbing in my ears, making my knees weak. Men and women are throwing aside books that are empty. The torchlight is dancing. In the shadows and orange light creating strange, twisting movements, my neighbors look more like creatures than people. Their clothes hang off of their thin frames. Their hungry eyes are wild.

"Such talismans are witchcraft, I say," Elias continues to shout. "Witchcraft!"

Scrolls are tossed in the air. Books slide across the floor. Scarlet would be upset by this.

"Here!" a woman shouts.

The search pauses. My heart skips a beat as she pulls something out of the pages of a book. From my distance, I can only tell that whatever she is holding is dark. I don't see the cream stripes of Lady's feathers.

"What is it?" Bram asks, stepping up to the woman.

I watch Elias for his reaction. His mouth is small and shriveled. Tight. Like his features. Like a dried mushroom.

"A lock of hair," the woman replies, sounding somewhat aston-ished. "Black hair."

Cavan's hand tightens on my bicep. He stands all the straighter.

"Scarlet," he whispers.

His hand is suddenly gone and he strides past me, stalking towards Elias. Geralt and Ethel close ranks around the village elder to shield him but Cavan peers at the older man over their shoulders.

"She thought Jasper had cut it in the night as some prank," he seethes. "But it was you... you..."

Elias shifts to conceal himself behind the siblings. His shoulders are hunched.

Without Cavan helping me stay upright, I should be sagging. But I'm not sagging. I stand all the taller. A fire has been lit in me now, reinvigorating my body.

Anger.

Because sometimes Scarlet would come home with a smudge of ink on her cheek. Ink because every once in a while she would fall asleep reading with her face on a book. The thought of that lecherous fiend touching her... cutting off some of her hair without her knowing... the knowing that it has been here all this time...

I want to hit him. I have never wanted to hit anyone so badly. I want my hand to ache from pummeling him.

A strange sort of quietness has settled in the room even as several continue to go through the shelves, searching for more evidence.

Cavan strides up to a shelf. With a roar, he swipes all of the books off of the wood. He stands there for a moment, panting as he gazes down at them then bends over to roughly shake their pages. I wish I could help him, but the blacksmith's grip is still firm. He is unconvinced.

Andrew is in the corner. He has been holding still for some time with his back to the room. While he was never cruel, he has been much more agreeable since the ale and cider ran out. In the dancing shadows I can see his arms moving, as if he is stroking his white beard that extends down to his chest. I watch him for some time, and eventually, Megan's mother also notices his odd behavior. She has been stacking discarded books in the center of the library, attempting some semblance of order.

"Andrew?" she asks, closing the book she has in her hands.

Though Andrew doesn't reply, he stops stroking his beard and I know he has heard her.

Megan's mother stands still in the middle of the room while the others hunt through the remaining books, speaking to each other in clipped voices. The elderly man slowly pivots to face the miller's wife. Even in the dimness, I can see that it wasn't his beard that he was stroking, after all. He was arranging a necklace over it. The necklace I made for my father.

She lets out a gasp, holding a hand to her mouth. That draws the attention of the others who look at Megan's mother, hoping she found something, then follow her gaze. Andrew shuffles into the light in the center of the room.

"Those are falcon feathers," Cavan announces. He pivots to peer at me over his shoulder, a mixture of pride, satisfaction, and terror in his stance. "Lady's feathers."

There is a moment that seems to last far longer than possible. It's as if I can feel the thoughts around me shifting. It's not that they are all looking at me, but I know the mud from when I was small is being cleaned off of my body in their eyes. For the first time, I notice that Megan is in the room with me. Her eyes are watering as she smiles at me, holding one of the torches. The harshness of the light illuminates the patches of scalp beneath her stiff, thin hair.

The strength that trickled into my limbs from my anger at Elias is now doubling. My mud is gone and I am standing tall. No one speaks. The torches hiss and snap. The blacksmith releases my arm. There is a tug on my wrists. He has cut the twine.

Before I or anyone has a chance to move or speak, Elias shoves Geralt and makes a mad dash for the door. I don't think. I bolt after him. He is surprisingly swift. His brown robes make a flapping sound, like a flag, as they flutter. I use their noise to guide me more than my vision, for without the torches, his dark clothing is difficult to make out.

I should not be doing this. I shouldn't be running. The world suddenly looks as if it's underwater. I feel as if I'm listing to the side, even though I know I am not. But I can't let him escape.

Elias darts past the stool he tried to use as an executioner's block. The knife is sitting on its seat. He scuttles to a slow when he catches sight of the blade but has to double back a few steps to reach it. Only he makes the mistake of looking up and seeing me. Though he lunges for the knife, he can't suppress a scream. He flutters back-wards as soon as he has the weapon, fleeing for the woods.

"Draven!"

Someone is shouting my name. They have been for some time. I had thought their voice was my heartbeat.

"Draven!"

I pass the stool.

"Draven Lucian's Son," the voice bellows, strained from exertion. "On behalf of your father, stop!"

For some reason, the request makes my heels skid across the gravel, slowing. I pivot to peer at the owner of the voice. It's Cavan. More are following behind him in the distance. There is a look on his face that should not be given to me. It should be given to Willow or Jasper, who I only now realize must have been taken home by his mother. Probably when she thought I was about to be killed.

Cavan slows to a jog as he closes the distance between us and the concern on his dark-bearded face makes my vision swim. I can't catch my breath. Then one of my legs gives out. I should hit the ground hard, but I don't. Cavan surges forward and manages to catch my torso.

I'm gasping for air. Hot and cold. Weak and full of a raging fire that wants me to run, run, run. To hunt, hunt, hunt. But arms are around me now, supporting my weight, and I can't seem to get my legs to move.

"Water," Cavan is shouting. "Bring him water!"

I only realize my eyes are closed when I notice that I can't see him. I force them to open and when his eyes meet mine, I realize for the first time that they have a hint of green in them, like hers.

"Willow..." I gasp. "Willow."

"I know, my boy," he whispers, squeezing whatever part of me he can. "I know."

Time passes. It must because I take so many sips of water. The world seems to fade in and out of my mind as Cavan holds me. I'm so relaxed against his chest and his heartbeat is so lulling that I could sleep. Maybe I do sleep, because each time he holds a cup to my lips and I can see and hear again, the people around me are doing different things. Arguing. Lighting lanterns. Gathering just a few yards from me. Watching me. So many eyes watching me.

They want Elias. They want Willow. They want justice.

Andrew crouches beside me. His feeble hands hold out the necklace I made for my father. I trail my fingers over the soft feathers. One has been bent crooked. In that moment, I can hear my father's laughter. The pride in his voice when he told me that Lady was mine after she hatched. The squeeze of his hand on my shoulder when she brought us her first rabbit. Lady's feathers were so soft. Like Scarlet's hair. Scarlet's hair that Elias stole because his stares weren't enough.

Fire. The fire is back. He must be destroyed.

I push myself off of Willow's father and he steadies me with his hands. It takes me a moment but I manage to stagger to my feet. The water and rest have done me some good. Though I feel slightly off balance, the world isn't listing as it was before.

The people of Morrot who have been meandering around all turn their attention to me. I see the ten that I armed, but there are more people than that. With surprise I notice my mother in the shadows. I haven't heard her voice or felt her touch, but then again, that is nothing new. The hollowness is back in her eyes as she toys with something in her hands. Andrew has given her the necklace.

Cavan holds something out to me. It's my hunting knife. They must've taken it when they forced me onto my knees. Then the black-smith presses something heavy into one of my palms. It's my crossbow. His eyes are both hard and soft. With a nod of thanks, I check that it's loaded then hook it on my belt where it belongs.

I face the woods. In the torchlight, I can see Elias' tracks. He won't have gone far. The woods are no place for a man like him. There is nothing he can control in the forest. I will flush him out like a fowl, for he is foul. I step towards the darkness.

People shout at me. Ask me where I am going. What I'm doing. What *they* should be doing.

I don't answer them. It's enough to train the burning muscles of my legs to walk again. Cavan answers for me.

"He is hunting."

I smile at that. I can't help it. Because in a way, I have been hunting Elias all my life.

# Chapter Ten

Light seems to trail after me, providing some dim illumination ahead as the villagers decide that they are coming with me. After all, I armed ten of them. But I am unused to light in the forest these days. I jog a little to shelter in the shadows. I know Willow's father is behind me, silently keeping track of my whereabouts the same way he does when we hunt together. Every once in a while I will break a twig or kick a rock to let him know where I am.

The woods are so cold. So incredibly cold. As I use my sleeve to wipe sweat off of my brow, I worry for the first time that I may be getting ill. But that is not for me to think about right now. Right now I have a quarry.

Finding Elias' trail is relatively easy. He's clumsy and has no idea where he is. It becomes all the easier when I hear him dart into the underbrush up ahead of me. I knew he would be resting, hiding somewhere nearby. I didn't expect him to be foolish enough to bolt when I got near. I give no sign that I have noticed him. Instead, I continue to pick my way along the game trail, listening to his movements.

In this way we pass hours. I'm sure Cavan thinks that I have a plan, but really the only strategy I have is to stalk up as close to the man as I can and gut him. Or beat him. Bludgeon him with a rock like he did to my father. Burn him alive like he did to Scarlet.

Narrowing my eyes, I force my focus back into my body and my surroundings, realizing that my fantasies of revenge have distracted me to the point that I let the torches get too close. I can see the outlines of some of the branches and rocks ahead. I pause, pivoting to gauge how far out my followers are. I can't see any of them. Only the pricks of their lanterns in the distance. Too far away to cast any illumination on me now.

If not from their lanterns... where is the light?

I look up. The sky is a dull shade of grey. It's enough to make me gasp. My legs tremble. I want to drop to my knees.

Darkness. Darkness is fading.

When I take a step, the silhouettes and shadows around me blur, but this time it isn't from my dizzy mind. It's because I am so full of something light and buoyant and beautiful that I'm crying. Hope. I am full of hope.

Tears drop from my lashes as I continue into the forest. The more I look, the more I see.

"Willow," I whisper past a smile. "Oh, Willow."

She has done it. She has defeated the Bringer of Darkness. She has saved us all.

A rock is kicked up ahead. Elias is using the increased visibility to put as much distance between us as he can. His clumsiness tells me exactly where he is.

We are alone. Even Cavan has fallen behind. All I have to do is sprint. I will have Elias at my mercy. I can hit. Kick. Smash his face in the mud. I can slash and torture. But now that I have it, now that the choice is mine, I no longer want it. Because the light is returning. Because Willow is a hero. But mostly because I *can*. I can do anything and nothing.

Elias makes a run for it. There is a clearing up ahead and I can make out his silhouette amidst the whiteness of the snow that wasn't stopped by the dead trees.

"With me," I shout, bewildered as to where the words have come from. "With me!"

I don't know if anyone has heard me, but I'm not wasting the time to find out.

If ever a person is alone in the wilds and encounters a predator, the last thing they should do is flee. Be it a wolf or bear or cat, the hunter's instinct will be triggered by the person's movement. Running away is the best means to get yourself killed. Instead, you ought to wave your arms to look bigger. Make loud noises. Climb a tree or hide if you must, but not run. Never run. But Elias is running and now so are my legs. I cannot stop myself.

I'm a hunter, and this is the end.

Shouts ring out behind me as I break into the clearing. Elias himself is screaming. The sounds only make me run all the faster, despite the fire eating at the edges of the wound in my neck. I know it's bleeding again but I couldn't slow now even if I wanted to. The coward is crying out for help as he enters another grove and I can see orange light in the distance.

Windows. A house. *The* house.

Figures are outside. One is almost invisible against the snow because of her white dress. Willow. Tristan. Elias is making his way towards them, his hands extended. Pleading. I can't make out what he is saying. In fact, I can't hear much of anything over the drum of my own pulse and my heaving lungs.

Elias trips and stumbles as he approaches. I search for my bees to shout at Tristan not to listen. Not to help. Then he punches Elias, knocking him over onto his back.

The tickle of laughter bounces up my stomach and into my throat so strongly that I begin to slow my pace. He knows. Tristan knows who Elias is. Of course he does. Willow will have told him. I slow to a walk completely when I can hear Tristan's roared words.

"She suffered for days!" He kicks Elias in the head, knocking the elder man onto his back.

"You heartless bastard."

When Willow latches onto Tristan's arm to restrain him, telling him that he is not a killer, I walk to them. The shouts behind me are closer now. The village is catching up. As I stride towards the house, I almost smile for I can make out the black and white of Tristan's vest and shirt. The gold of Willow's curls. The dirt of her dress.

The sight of Elias on the ground, helpless, makes me break into a lope. He is weak. Old. I withdraw my crossbow. My quarry is cornered. A stillness settles over me as Willow and Tristan turn their backs on Elias, leaving the old man in the cold. There is no escape for my prey. I have only to—

With a wild scream, Elias gets to his feet and charges, brandishing a knife. He is going to hurt one of them. My crossbow is raised before I can finish my thought. My heels skid in the dusting of snow beneath me as I halt, aim, and release the bolt. I hit my mark of Elias' wrist, disarming him. The elder man wrenches his arm back as he lets out a cry.

In my peripheral, I see Willow and Tristan turn to face me as Elias topples. I lower my crossbow then drop it in favor of my knife. I stride towards him before I even know what I am doing. I cannot see an aging man. I cannot see a person at all. Only darkness.

Elias is whimpering, clutching his bleeding wrist and trying to drag his wounded form away from me.

"No, no please. Please, boy," he pleads.

I place a foot on either side of his robes and bend over. My body feels as if it is moving on its own. I adjust the grip on my knife and yank the blade across Elias' throat. His pleading dissolves into gurgles. Blood rushes out and the noises stop. I wipe my knife on my sleeve and rise as Elias' body slumps, going limp. Limp because he can no longer move his eyes to look at young women. His hands to cut their hair. His arms to murder.

Dead. Elias is dead. And I have killed him.

I have killed a man.

Snow crunches in a pattern behind me. Villagers are approaching. Everything is so bright. I sheathe my knife and pivot to face the people of Morrot as they approach. Several slow when they see what I have done. The red staining the snow.

There is suddenly so much brilliance in the world and in the hearts beating around me that anything and everything feels possible. I feel light. I feel—

*Twang.*

Someone has fired a crossbow. I saw the movement out of the corner of my eye and twist my pained neck to see who has fired.

*Thud.*

The sound of a bolt sticking into flesh.

My mother's holding the weapon but it's not aimed at Elias' body. It's aimed at Tristan. She screams as she lowers the weapon. She has shot him. Him. The man with Willow. The man Willow adores. Her mother's wedding dress is splattered with blood. I see her holding Tristan's waist, falling to the ground with him as I charge my mother, bellowing. I don't even know what word I'm saying until I repeat it again.

"No!"

I yank the crossbow from her hands. Her eyes and body are stiff with shock, staring at the man dying in Willow's arms. I hurl the weapon as far away from my mother as I can manage, but the act sends my vision into a spiral. Suddenly I'm spinning, falling into Willow's lament. She is making the most horrible choking sounds. Her head is on Tristan's chest. He isn't moving.

My mother has killed him.

My mother has killed a man.

Cavan tries to hold his daughter as she weeps. To gather her up in his arms. To comfort her. Lead her away. My sight of them is blurred by my tears.

"Why?" I whisper to my mother as she wails. Megan's mother wraps her arms around her. I turn to face the two older women, tears clearing my vision as they fall. "Why?"

"He was a monster," my mother moans. "A monster. I didn't know he was a man. Not a man."

Megan's mother does her best to support her as she sinks to her knees.

Willow is screaming. Her father has an arm around her waist, hoisting her up. Leading her away from the body. Her cries sear at my thoughts, setting them on fire. In their ashes, I know that she loved Tristan dearly. She sees my mother as she passes. Then me.

Our eyes meet, only I can't see her clearly because mine are filled with tears again. She stops resisting her father. We have not seen each other in the light since we were children. Now all that lies between us is grief. Such terrible, insurmountable grief.

Cavan pulls Willow close then hoists her into his arms.

Megan's mother leads my mother away. Snow crunches around me as villagers either head back to Morrot or approach the house. Tristan's house. No one else approaches his body, so I do.

My legs ache and burn. I once more feel as if I'm floating but I cannot fight the sensation anymore. I study Tristan's still face as I near. There are marks on his cheek. Red, corded, pained marks that weren't there before. Burns covering half of his face. The half my mother saw. Monster.

"I am sorry," I whisper. His eyes are mere filmy slits beneath a fan of dark lashes. "So very sorry."

Tears are warming my cheeks. My cheeks that are so cold. The door of the house bangs open as people poke their heads inside. Others are venturing into the remnants of the garden where Victoria held me prisoner. The rest have left, following Willow's family.

Droplets of blood have sunken into the thin layer of snow. I wonder if they will become ice.

"We must bury him," I whisper to no one.

Lifting my head, I nearly lose my footing and have to hold out an arm to balance myself. A handful of people are still within earshot, so I raise my voice and shout for the third time in my life.

"Who will help me bury this man?"

The villagers milling about the house and trees stare at me as if I have lost my mind.

Then I will do it myself.

Crouching, I slide Tristan's arm around my shoulders and slip one of my arms under his torso, intending to carry him like a deer. Though he was smaller than me in life, he is heavy. I groan, straining as I try to shift his weight onto my back. One of my boots slips in the snow. I cry out in frustration. I am so weak. So very weak.

Then thin pale, freckled arms peeking out of long sleeves wrap around Tristan's waist.

"Megan," I gasp around a small smile.

She returns the expression, her eyes sunken in her gaunt face. In the light I can see just how old starvation has made her look. I'm sure I am just as worse for wear.

"I will help you, Draven," she says. "I will help you."

Together, we struggle and strain. Then the blacksmith exits the house and helps us, as well. I won't bury Tristan at the house. Not near Victoria. I have a different place in a mind. Somewhere beautiful and quiet. Somewhere Willow will be able to visit.

Neither Megan nor the blacksmith ask where we are going. They dutifully help me bear his weight. Weight. He is so heavy. Everything is so heavy, pushing me down into the ground. The world is so bright. I am so cold. And then the ground is coming closer and closer. Blinding white snow. Megan yelps. I know that I have fallen once the cold and grit press into my cheek, but that is the last thing I know.

"Watch the eddies," my father cautions.

He has our fishing net slung over his shoulder. His dark eyes seem to dance in the sunlight. When he is happy like this, they remind me of the light bouncing around on the water in the river at my side. They make me laugh. The skin around his eyes crinkles as he grins. He ruffles my hair before he continues.

"The surface of the water is misleadingly smooth, but in the eddies, you can glimpse the true strength of the current. Watch."

He snatches a twig up off of the sandy river bank and tosses it onto the somewhat placid surface. It's swept away so swiftly that I almost lose sight of it. I grab my father's hand that's twice the size of

mine and he gives it a reassuring squeeze. I'm not really that frightened but I press my body to the side of his leg all the same because
doing so makes me feel good. Sheltered. Wanted.

For a few moments, there is only my father's strong presence, the
warming of the sunlight on our backs, and the babbling of the water
that blends with the birdsong in the trees that surround us. The
breeze flutters the leaves making a gentle hissing noise, like a whisper. I step over to a grove of alder trees, watching the pale green of the
leaves, yellowed with sunlight, tracing their silhouetted veins with
my eyes.

Whisper, yes. The leaves whisper.

"Draven..." they say. "Draven..."

I take a few more measured steps towards them. Behind me, I
know that my father is wandering the bank, eyeing the stones he can
step on to reach the pool in the bend of the river where he will sink
our net. But right now, it is only me and the alders.

The leaves twist and flutter, like the rounded tips of spears, and
the smell of standing in the coolness beneath them... Oh, the smell!
It's a mix of spice and sweet, like a tea formed from the leaves and the
damp sand and jumbled driftwood amidst their trunks. I wend my
way through the fallen logs and boughs and tangled roots. The leaves
coo as I do so, talking amongst themselves.

"There he is," they say.

"The boy who does not speak?"

"The silent child."

"I am not silent," I say as I catch sight of something white peeking
out of the tangled roots. It looks like a shard of ceramic. There are
often treasures swept downstream from other people.

My father peers at me over his shoulder, as if doubting that he
heard me speak at all, then returns his attention to surveying the
deep pool.

"We don't mind," the trees continue. "We like the quiet."

"Not a silent boy, then. Just a broken boy. A very broken boy."

I pick up the shard of ceramic and am delighted to see that the
opposite side is painted with delicate blue designs. It was once a

piece of a plate. The only painted shape I can clearly make out is a wagon wheel. Maybe some grass...

"I am not broken," I whisper.

"Oh, but you are," the alders insist, their voices growing louder amidst a stronger gust of wind. "You are the rabbit's child. The rabbit's child. The acorn and the thistle down."

"No thistle," I breathe, running my fingertips over the river-smoothed edge of the shard.

"Eyes as black as the deep, deep earth," they wail. "Eyes like bark and coal."

I peer up at the alders, watching as their leaves flutter and slide against each other with little hisses and sighs. No one else ever seems to understand their words.

"The earth?" I whisper-ask.

"Broken boy," they croon. "Broken boy, you are the rabbit's child."

"The acorn," one wails.

"And the thistle down," another moans.

The teasing song surrounds me. I rise, spinning in a slow circle to watch their slithering, haloed dance above.

"You are the rabbit's child."

"The acorn."

"And the thistle down."

They are growing louder and I can no longer feel the sunlight amidst the steady breeze. Gooseflesh ripples across my arms and back.

"Draven?" my father calls. His voice sounds so far away.

"The rabbit's child."

I drop the piece of plate. Broken. Like me. But I don't know why.

"Acorn..."

A gust kicks up so strong that it whistles through the swaying boughs, drowning out the sounds of the nearby water.

"Thistle down..."

My heart is hammering in my breast as if it could burst. I hop and weave. Burrow and climb. Like a rabbit. I need my father. My father...

The laughter of the alders trails after me as I break out from under their canopy.

"Quiet boy."

"Beloved boy."

"Come back to us now."

"Come back..."

The sand grinds beneath my boots as I run for my father. He is several yards off, perched on a rock amidst the sparkling water, using a branch to reposition parts of the net he has already cast. I make for him, splashing through the shallows and hopping up onto bigger rocks that make the river as good as shallow.

My father twists to peer at me with worry. My father whose eyes are dark, but not like mine. My father whose face is very lined. My father who says that I take after my mother, because I don't look a thing like him. Willow's father traded for a mirror last summer. It rests in Cavan's workroom where he stores his goods for trade. I have seen my reflection. My father is right. But he is also wrong.

A sorrow deep and cold surges up in me. I let out a wail before the tears even come.

"Draven," my father calls, turning to face me as I leap onto another rock and nearly lose my footing. "What happened? Were you stung?"

"Papa," I cry, holding my arms out to him as I hop to the next rock beside his. Only this time, I do lose my footing. My father isn't fast enough. I fall sideways into the river. The force of the frigid water pummeling my body coughs all of the air from my lungs and I can't move. No, I can move. The river is moving me but I cannot move myself.

My father is screaming my name. Any moment now I will feel the pain of his tight hands around my arms, hoisting me out of the danger. Any moment now...

His hands don't come. They don't come because I remember that my father is dead. Lucian is dead. And I am not a child. Not a child... I am a man, a head taller than my father ever was, and this is just a memory. A memory of the day that I was taunted by trees and slipped into the water. Father pulled me out. He carried me to shore. He stripped off my wet clothing and told me to lie in the warm sand. He sang funny songs to calm me. He didn't let me drown.

Then why am I drowning now?

The rush of the water is surrounding me and the cold numbs me to the rocks and branches scraping at my skin. I can't breathe. I can't move. I can't do anything but spin and drift.

Voices. There are voices. A man.

"Papa?"

He stops speaking.

"Draven?" a woman asks.

I know that voice. My mother.

The river isn't carrying me so swiftly anymore. I can focus. I can feel the prick of the straw in my mattress. The stickiness of damp fur against my bare skin. My bed. My room. My home. I'm not in the water at all. The rushing sound is the blood in my ears.

A hand is on my shoulder, giving a gentle squeeze. She's speaking again so I open my eyes because I know I heard my father and I haven't seen him for so very long. Not since he died.

The room is dim. Of course it is. No, wait. Night. This is night. Night because the darkness was lifted. Willow is a hero. I can just make out the curve of her cheekbone and ear in the firelight. The more I blink, the lighter the room seems to become. I can see her face now. She is smiling down at me. I twist my neck to look behind her but am filled with such a searing pain that I hiss, certain that someone has just dropped a burning coal onto my throat.

"Lay still," the man cautions. "Just rest."

It takes some time for the fire to subside enough for me to see again, but when it does, I am able to think clearly. That's not my father's voice at all. It's Cavan's. Willow's father. Not my father... not my father...

Because I am the rabbit's child. The acorn and the thistle down.

"Thistle..." I whisper.

My mother asks me to repeat what I said but my eyelids are so heavy. I cannot bear the weight of my own chest. My own being. So I let go.

# Chapter Eleven

Watched. I am being watched. When next I wake, my Watcher is there beside me in her white gown.

Beside me? No, no, I don't want her here. She takes. She takes and takes and takes.

I want to tell her to go. That I know she is Victoria. That she will get nothing from me ever again. But I cannot part my lips or find my bee-letters. I cannot make a sound. I'm a prisoner in my own body, completely at her mercy. Helpless. Alone. In the dark. So much darkness, even though the light has returned. So much darkness...

A light. And suddenly I am light. My arms are no longer heavy and I can move my legs. Lift my head. I'm standing in the middle of a parlor and a lamp is burning on a low table in the center. It's just bright enough to cast a yellowed glow around the room, allowing me to recognize my surroundings. Two armchairs facing a hearth, a staircase behind them, a kitchen just beyond. It is Tristan's parlor, only everything about it feels different. While the chairs still have their holes and the fireplace still has its moss, nothing smells dusty or damp or close. Like a coffin. In fact, there are no smells, at all. No heat or cold. Only sight and sound.

A low, sucking boom startles me from behind. The fire in the hearth has sprung to life. I'm distracted by it long enough to not notice someone else in the room with me. Someone who had been hiding in the shadows. Now I hear the scuff of shoes.

No. No, this is where she attacked me. Where she hurt me. I cannot go through that again. I cannot have any more kisses tainted with hatred. Any more caresses stained with pain. I cannot have any more of *her* at all.

My hand darts up to my neck to shield my wound, but all my palm finds is solid skin. No hole. No burning. No death spot.

"Draven."

I stand a little taller. When I turn around I let my hand fall aside. I am not alone with Victoria. Instead, Tristan gazes at me from across the parlor, the dancing light of the fire reflecting in his brown eyes that smile softly. His hands are in the pockets of his black trousers and his shoulders are slightly slumped. Relaxed. Not at all like the first time I came into his house.

"I thought you were..." I begin.

"I know. But fear not. Victoria is..." he pauses to inhale a deep breath. His eyes dart up to the room at the end of the hall upstairs then sweep across the ceiling. "Well, she is certainly not here. She has moved on. Left the Netherworld."

There is so much in his words for me to absorb that I relax my mind. Something in me tells me that I don't have to understand it all, just as I still don't understand everything that happened the last time I was inside this house. As if it all occurred in a different time and space. Maybe it did. Nothing much makes sense anymore.

Tristan lets out a little huff. "Dearie me, where are my manners?"

He bustles over to the armchairs and arranges them so that they are facing each other, then glances up at me through dark bangs that have fallen into his face. It's only then that I realize half of his face is covered in twisted, red scars, unlike the first time that I met him. I don't know why, but the sight of them makes me trust him as if I had known him all my life.

"Some refreshment?"

I incline my head. "Thank you."

Tristan flashes a smile before stepping lively into the kitchen, lamps illuminating in his path, lighting the house. I can't help but smirk at the sight, but it isn't only the lights that are making me lift inside. I have never called on anyone before and been offered something to eat or drink, other than by Willow and her family.

One of the armchairs is waiting for me so I sink into its mice-eaten cushions. While I wait, I let my gaze wander. The walls are covered in what used to be wallpaper but are now just a mildewed, peeling mess. There are odd stains on the floor. Cobwebs still flutter in the highest corners. The corners that Willow couldn't reach, for shrouded in darkness or not, she would never have spent so much time in a filthy house. The idea of her attempting to tidy up this place, like some lost princess in one of Scarlet's stories, makes me laugh softly.

My host returns with two goblets full of cold water which he sets on the low table beside the armchairs.

"My apologies but I haven't much else to offer."

"It's enough that you have offered me something at all," I mutter.

Tristan tugs up the waist of his trousers then takes a seat across from me. "You're not very highly thought of in your village, are you?"

"I can't blame them. They can all speak so much that they toss words into the air like petals at a wedding. Something pretty and frivolous to be stepped on. Words to them come so easy. They don't have to struggle or fight or... or fear."

"Fear?" he asks before leaning forward to grab his goblet, droplets of water clinging to the outside of the cup, jetting down to the stem at his touch.

"Well, I never know when my quietness is going to anger someone."

"Humph," he commiserates as he takes a sip.

"Or when I will say the wrong thing."

"But you can talk to Willow?"

"Of course," I nod, mimicking him and grabbing my own goblet for a sip. The water is cool and tasteless.

"Because she has never been angry with you?"

I snort as I finish my sip. "I wouldn't go that far."

Tristan lets out a laugh that is more of a bark which teases out my own. It's only then that I realize how easy this all is. My words are not a struggle. My wound is gone. Tristan is so welcoming.

How did I get here?

The smile hasn't quite left my face as I glance around again with bemusement. When my gaze returns to Tristan's, he is watching me with eyes that remind me of Lady's. So sharp and focused. My smile fades as I trace the lines of his black vest over his white shirt. No blood. No hole from the crossbow bolt. He follows my gaze and seemingly my thoughts and runs a hand over his heart where he received his mortal wound.

"I was trapped," he begins softly. "Victoria, my wife—"

"We've met," I can't hold back.

"Yes, yes, of course. Let me begin again." He takes a moment to study his hands, biting his lower lip. "I met your father once when he was out hunting. I had hoped that he and I would become friends. That we could conduct trades." He then lifts his eyes to peer at me through his bangs. "More than supplies, I needed an escape. My wife, well... she wasn't ever well. I needed other people. Other places. Anything other than her suffocating presence."

He shakes his head, as if breaking out of a hold on his very thoughts. I remember her sweetness. Her seduction. Her teeth, tearing, tearing, tearing. I set aside my goblet to try to disguise a shudder.

"My father told Elias, and Elias killed him," I explain to Tristan. "He couldn't take the risk of anyone else from the village meeting you. Of Morrot learning from you instead of from him."

Tristan nods gravely. He swipes a hand over the scarred side of his face, brushing aside his bangs for at least a few seconds as he leans back in his armchair, his eyes dull. "Then Scarlet discovered his guilt and he also killed her to avoid being exposed."

I can't bring myself to nod. Even though it has been more than a year, I sometimes think the smoke has stained my nostrils.

"But what you may not know is that he tried to eliminate the threat all together."

I furrow my brows. "Eliminate?"

Tristan studies me for the length of several heartbeats and as the light dances across the corded, polished skin of his scars, I realize that I have never before wondered where they came from. His eyes drift to the flames, and for some time, he is lost in his own thoughts. I allow him this space.

If there is one thing I understand, it's not having words when you want them.

"He poured resin down our chimney in our bedchamber so that when I lit it, well..." He gestures a hand towards the flames and then upwards. He doesn't need to say more. "Victoria was so badly burned that she begged me to end her life." Tristan meets my gaze with his next words. "So I did."

At first it's difficult to hold his gaze, but then it becomes as easy as breathing.

"Only the cut of my knife wasn't the end. She lingered here, as a corpse. When she died, she took a part of my spirit with her, trapping me in-between life and the Netherworld. She fed on me to keep her body... well, functional, though that was sometimes up for debate as she tended to get rather..." He makes his eyes go crooked and his jaw hangs at an angle, his arms floppy. I laugh softly. "And so I was her prisoner for years, tortured almost daily while she siphoned all of the light from the woods and then from the entire valley."

"Until Willow."

"Yes," he says on an exhale, and her name transforms his face so much that he almost looks like a different man. His eyes become unfocused and alight and a flush enters his unmarked cheek, filling it with life. He speaks around a small smile. "Yes, until Willow."

I expect a pang in my chest. A flutter of grief. After all, was I not so wounded when I thought Willow was with Scott? When I first realized how much she cared for Tristan over me? Instead, I only feel a calm hum in my chest, like the reflection of happiness. Because Willow had happiness, however brief, and so did Tristan.

*Did.* Yes, of course, Tristan is dead. So how can I be talking with him?

"She changed everything, you know," Tristan continues, folding a leg over a knee. "This house. My thoughts. She was like…"

"A light in the dark."

"Yes, exactly." He smiles as he rests his chin on his knuckles, his elbow propped on the arm of his chair, his eyes gazing into the flames of the fire, full of warm reverie. "I never knew what strength I had until I met her. I never understood what it was to give without any expectation of receiving. It was the first time that I had ever truly…"

He falters.

"That I…"

"Loved," I finish for him.

"Yes," he agrees softly, shifting to study his hand that he had been propping his chin on. "Yes." When he meets my gaze, there is pain in the lines around his eyes and his mouth and I know it is not all his. He knows who I am. Who knows who she was to me.

*Was.* Yes, was. Not is.

"Victoria… she saw the difference. She knew that what she was doing was wrong. So in the end, she allowed herself to let go of her fear and move beyond the Netherworld."

My brows lower. "What's beyond the Netherworld?"

Tristan shakes his head the slightest bit then busies himself straightening his vest. "I wouldn't know. I haven't been there yet, myself. That's why I am able to visit with you like this. All I know is that there is no coming back from what lies beyond."

I nod slowly, feeling my thoughts shift and make room for this new world order. For the thought of a "beyond" that is a mystery even to the dead.

"And no, you are not yet a spirit like me," Tristan suddenly assures, his eyes once again sharp and present. "Close, but not dead. You are still gallantly fighting for your life because of that ghastly wound my ex-wife gave to you. Ha-ha! Did you hear that?" he squawks with sudden joy. "*Ex*-wife. That's right; I believe I have grounds to justify a divorce."

"And then some."

He lets out a soft giggle, as if enjoying this newfound identity. "I really do wish we had some wine."

"Aren't we not really here in body?"

He shrugs and takes a sip of his water. "Let's leave those pesky little details out of this."

"But I am actually still lying in my bed... dying?"

Tristan eyes me for a moment, biting his lower lip. "Willow has done her best to help you. I used to be an apothecary so I steered her in the right herbal direction, as it were."

My brows shoot up. "Of course. She's a Listener. She can still hear you. So... you don't have to be dead. To her. You can still—"

He waves his hand. "No."

"No?"

"No."

"But why not? If you two can still speak together, if you can still spend time in each other's company even without you having a body, then why not at least try?"

"Because it is wrong."

"Nothing about it is wrong. You make her happy."

Tristan arches a brow. "And you want her to be happy?"

"More than anything."

He studies me for some time, letting the words we have just spoken hang in the air between us, dancing on the shadows and light cast into the room from the fire. At length, a small smile spreads across his lips and I realize that what I thought was just a reflection of the firelight is actually admiration in his eyes.

"And there we have it," he softly announces.

"And there we have what?"

He lets out a soft chuckle and shakes his head with a coyness that makes me shift in my chair. He takes another sip of water. "She often spoke about you, you know."

"We grew up together," I evenly reply.

"You have always been a good friend to her."

I nod. "I'm glad. I have tried."

Tristan bites his lower lip, appraising me for some time again as he slowly nods, as if expecting me to grasp at something that our words have left in the air.

"So the darkness has lifted now," he announces, setting his goblet on the table and shifting his weight to get more comfortable. "What will you do?"

I shrug one shoulder. "I think that's a little premature, don't you?"

"Why?"

"You said it yourself, I am dying, and that's why you and I are... visiting."

"No, I said you were gallantly fighting for your life and that Willow has done her best to help you heal."

I screw my eyes shut. "Then let's trade places."

"What?" he squeaks.

I open my eyes. "My life for yours."

Tristan blinks several times, his lips parted. "You would do that?"

"Yes."

He scoots forward in his chair and his brown eyes are the only thing I can see in the room. "You would forsake what could be fifty more years on earth, right this minute, for me?"

I nod. "And for her, yes."

"There would be no going back."

"I understand."

"And once you leave the Netherworld—"

"You can't tell me what would happen, I know. So can it be done?"

Tristan smiles sadly. "Of course not."

I let out a hiss and lean back in my chair, arching my neck in frustration. "Then stop wasting your time with me. Go spend it with her. *Talk* to her. Let her know—"

"I can't."

"You just said that you told her how to help me."

"Then I *will* not," Tristan amends.

"But why?"

"Because she would be my prisoner," he whispers.

I shake my head. "That's ridiculous. She would be—"

"Chained to whispers it takes nearly everything in me to form.

Chained to a memory of a touch she can never have. A man who was only ever half there to begin with."

"It would be her *choice*," I counter.

Tristan shakes his head, his bangs falling into his dark eyes again. His voice is soft. "It would make me Victoria."

"You could *never* be like her," I firmly reply.

"I would be blinding her from life and all of its joys. I would be exactly like Victoria. And that is so, so far from what I want for Willow."

Something he has said reminds me of Lady. Of how I never could notice Megan when Willow was near. How I was a shadow. "Is not everyone devoted also blinded? Don't we all forget the rest of the world because of this one light? She would be just as blinded if you were there with her in body."

One brow twitches upwards. "I never blinded her from you, Draven."

"What?" I gasp.

He shakes his head. "Love does not make us so oblivious as to forget those we cherish deeply." Tristan clears his throat softly. "No, no I could never exist as a whisper and a memory. I want Willow to dance and laugh. To play and kiss and... well. She can't do any of that with me. And I have had my chance. More than one chance at life, actually. I am ready."

"Ready?"

As he nods, I notice for the first time that he doesn't seem to be many years older than me at all. "I have lived my life, Draven. It is time for you to live yours."

"I am."

"No, you have not been living. You have been surviving. There is a difference."

"I've never had much choice."

"You do now."

With that, he rises. I do, as well. He smiles at me for a moment, his hands in his trouser pockets, and I realize that this is goodbye. "Tristan..."

"Draven." He bobs his head the slightest bit. "Such a unique name. Where does it come from?"

"I don't know. Maybe nowhere."

"I somewhat doubt that. Everyone comes from somewhere, you know, and there are a lot of somewheres out there beyond Morrot." He extends his hand. "Goodbye, Draven. I really do wish you nothing but the best."

"As do I." I clasp his hand and don't let go once he tries to tug his free. "Must you?"

"No. There is no must. This is a want. I *want* to."

Though I cannot completely understand his decision, I slowly nod. His eyes flick to the entryway so I take a step towards it.

"Tristan?" I say as I suck in a breath, pausing to study him one last time. "Thank you."

He nods with a smile and I make my way to the door. I reach for the lever but pause when his voice sounds behind me.

"Oh, and Draven, one last thing to keep in mind."

I peer at him over my shoulder. The scarred half of his face is in shadows, the clear skin of the other half of his face softly hugged by the warm light. There is something so effortlessly endearing about him that I wish we could visit longer. That we had known each other better in life.

"A Listener can only hear the dead. You both saw Victoria because she was an abomination clinging to her corpse. In a meadow this morning, when I taught Willow what herb might save you, I was able to manipulate mist so that she might see my shape in life. But other than that, a Listener cannot see the spirits of the dead."

"No one can," I softly reply.

His lips press together the slightest bit as he appraises me for a moment. Then another. And another. The knowing look in his eye pierces my thoughts and I want to ask him what he means when I realize that I cannot move my mouth at all anymore. I cannot move anything. I'm back in my bed, covered in sweat and heat and cold and sticky deer pelts.

The hole in my neck is burning. I can't stop my limbs from twitching. My throat from vibrating with moans. Hands are on me, touching me, holding me down. A voice is calling to me, weeping. Weeping.

Why is there so much weeping in the world? Why is my Watcher, Victoria, here if she has moved on? I cannot say when my eyes are open or closed but I can see her in the gloom of our cabin, pacing in front of the fire, pinching her lips with her fingers as my mother tries to calm me. Her white gown. Her white gown.

# Chapter Twelve

The next time I'm aware, everything aches. I feel as if Aiken has taken his hammer and bruised every muscle in my body. But Aiken is dead and I am not beaten, I'm ill. Though I'm lying down, there is no comfort. Taking a few steady breaths, I await my mind to fully awaken. I can smell the sweat and leather of my bed. Hear the crackle and hiss of the fire that sounds far bigger than it ought to be. We shouldn't be wasting so much fuel.

Someone shifts a bowl on our wooden table. A throat clears absently. My mother. Her everyday noises make me feel more at peace than the comforts of the finest bed ever could.

I crack my eyes open and am surprised by the brightness of the world. Grey light illuminates our cabin. For the first time in over a year, I can properly see the interior, and it's somewhat embarrassing. Cobwebs adorn nearly every corner and the window panes are dulled with soot and fat from occasionally burning rushlights in our feeble attempt to spare our candles and oil lamps.

Something else is odd. I blink several times to make sense of what I am seeing, willing my bleary eyes to focus. Baskets line the wall by the door. Inside them are furs and pieces of wood. Tools. Carvings. They aren't ours and I wonder how they got here.

My mother steps out from behind the curtain of her bedroom, turning the upright boom in her hands and eyeing the bristles that I realize are covered in cobwebs. She has been cleaning. After a glance as she enters the main room, she looks at me again then drops the broom. She holds perfectly still as she gazes at me, as if afraid to trust her vision as much as I am, for there's light in our home. So much light.

She steps over to me quickly and immediately places a hand on my head. "You are not so warm," she gasps on an exhale then shifts to place both hands on my cheeks. Her palms press into hair that shouldn't be there for it hasn't been that long since I shaved, has it? "Not so warm at all."

Her pale eyes race over my face and hair, hands and neck as a smile blooms on her gaunt face, making her look younger than she has in years.

"Oh, my boy. Oh, my beautiful boy."

She brings one of my hands up to her lips and kisses my knuckles again and again. Something slides down my wrist as she does so. It's a bracelet made from dried, braided grass. A bracelet made by Willow, just as she did when we were small. She has been here.

I part my lips and try to speak. I try to vibrate my throat to ask a dozen questions, but even if I had my entire hive at my disposal, I still wouldn't have been able to speak. I can barely lift my arm. So instead, I let my eyes slip closed as my mother strokes my damp hair. Soon, I sleep.

The scratch of a beard on my temple. Arms slung under mine, around my chest. Someone is hoisting me up. It makes my head swim. The man is keeping me upright as someone arranges the pillows and furs behind me. My head slumps against the man's. He smells familiar but I know he is not my father because my father is dead, like Tristan and Scarlet and Victoria and Elias. I hope he is nowhere near those final two.

"That's it," the man is saying softly as he continues to support my weight. "That's it, brave boy."

He gently leans my body back against the stuffing and I realize that I'm now sitting up. Though my eyes are somewhat open, everything is so bright and blurry. Sluggishly, I realize that the people around me are my mother and Cavan. They are talking to each other and I really wish they would stop because I am so tired. I feel as if I haven't slept in days and my head is too heavy to keep up. I let it thump against a fur behind me.

"But that was three days ago," my mother says.

"He hasn't been conscious at all since?" Cavan asks.

"Sometimes he opens his eyes, but conscious? No."

This is foolishness. I was just awake. And I haven't slept at all, much less for three days.

"Is the water heated?"

My mother's feet scuff against the wood of the floor as she steps over to the fireplace. "Yes."

"Good. Good, good."

I'm having trouble catching my breath after all the moving. My heart is racing. Like a rabbit's. I am the rabbit's child. What're they doing?

Cavan is pouring something out of a wax-sealed jar and into a cup of steaming water.

"We must wait for it to cool," she cautions.

"Of course. I would add milk if there were any to be had."

"This is more than enough," my mother assures him with a thankful glance. "I didn't know there was even an ounce of honey left anywhere."

"No one did," Cavan agrees, pulling a chair away from the table and sinking into it. In the light, I can see just how lined and hollowed his face is. All the same, his body no longer has that strained look of being on the brink. As if he has eaten.

If three days passed since I was last awake and it only felt like moments to me, then how much time has passed since the return of the light?

"Old Andrew saw another discover it in Elias' quarters. When he realized it could help Draven, he confronted them and brought it to me."

My mother has gone rigid and is scrutinizing Cavan. She stiffly stirs the mug of hot water and honey before adding a bit more of the golden liquid. "Who had it?" she asks softly.

"That's not important anymore," Cavan sighs.

"Who *hoarded* it?"

Cavan keeps his gaze on my mother until she feels his eyes and returns the look. His expression is tired. Sad. He shakes his head, his voice soft. "We cannot do this. We cannot hold grudges over desperate deeds done in desperate times."

"Salmon," my mother insists. "Scott Stewart's Son was hoarding salmon jerky even after the lottery was announced. The lottery that was going to end my son's *life*."

"I would say that fate caught up with him, wouldn't you, Gwen?"

She stirs in the new honey a bit too violently and the haggard look on Willow's father's face tells me that he has had this conversation before.

"The trading party is due to return with cattle any day now. It does no one any good to dwell on past grievances and to fear what may come."

That seems to silence her and she dips a pinky tip in the drink. "It is cool enough, I think."

Cavan nods and looks at me as he rises, only to pause once he is upright. My mother follows his gaze. Neither knew that I was awake. Cavan's face grows more lined as he grins. I never noticed that he had lost a tooth or two in the back.

"Well, well, well, there's a shade of brown I haven't seen for some time."

I smile the slightest bit. I want to hug him. To thank him. But a twist of my lips is all I can manage.

Both cross over to me and I can practically feel my mother restraining herself from touching me. Guilt sours what's left of my stomach and creeps up my throat. I'm sorry that I have so frightened her.

"You must drink, do you understand?" he asks, easing into a crouch beside my bed. "Buds are on the trees. Grass is springing up everywhere. The squirrels and rats are returning. Everyone else has had something to eat. You have been very sick, do you understand?"

Why wouldn't I understand? Aren't I the one imprisoned in my own tortured body? I don't like the way Cavan's speaking to me as if I am simple. He has never been like the other parents in the village. He has never treated me as if I'm a dullard until now. The flicker of indignation gives me a strength I don't truly feel I have and I'm able to nod.

He chuckles softly. "What a scowl."

I didn't even realize I was making a face, but then again, I never seem to. So often my expressions speak for me without my bidding.

My mother rubs the back of my hand as Cavan holds the cup up to my lips. The water is sweet and warm. The honey soothes my throat. The hole in my neck aches as I swallow, which makes me only take little sips, but it's then that I realize how little my wound has pained me. It's healing.

Enough time passes for the shadows in the room to shift before I finally finish the cup, but neither my mother nor Willow's father show any hint of impatience. I don't know if it's the water or the honey, but it doesn't take long for my aching muscles to begin to calm. My chest isn't so heavy. I can shift my head.

After Cavan leaves, my mother scrapes a mixture of crushed thyme onto my wound, being as gentle as possible. "Willow brings me as much as she can find foraging each day. It's surprising how quickly plants grow once they have water and sunlight. The soil is so rich. It has had years of mulch."

I do my best to try to hide the pain she is causing by scraping the herb into my wound. Instead, I focus on her words. Willow. She spends every day looking for a means to save me because she is my friend and I am hers. I fall asleep with that simple thought and it warms me.

I have sunlight. A mother. Friendship.

The honey helps me tremendously. I drink as much of the mixture as I can over the next several days. Somehow I am always asleep when Willow comes by, or maybe she just waits until she knows I'm resting before entering. On the fifth day after my waking, I notice a braided bracelet made from fresh strands of grass on my wrist. I hold it up to my nose often, closing my eyes and inhaling the scent of life.

One afternoon, I hear a chicken squawking amidst the falling rain. The high pitch is so familiar that I almost don't take any notice until I remember that our last hen died ages ago. Now we have a new one. The trading party must have returned.

We are saved! We are saved.

That night, my mother gives me eggs and milk. I can't think about where she tells me they came from. That others are waiting for more hens and more milk but that there was a unanimous vote to give the first of both to me.

Me. Draven Who Does Not Speak.

The following morning, it's still raining. Someone is humming. The tune is familiar. It's "Midsummer's Song." The voice doesn't belong to my mother.

"Willow," I exhale before I even open my eyes.

The humming stops. Her warm hand slips into mine, giving it a gentle squeeze. I open my eyes for nothing other than the promise of her smile. Though I have to blink to clear my vision, she is a vision. Her yellow, curling hair seems piled around her head in an untidy heap and her sea-green eyes seem all the brighter with her smile. At first I think it is a trick of my bleary eyes, but it isn't. She has a few freckles. Sunlight has already decorated her skin.

"It is so good to see you," she whispers before bending over and kissing my hand held in hers.

See me? But hasn't she been to see me, every day, bringing the herbs?

She sniffles as she straightens and I realize that not only does she have tears in her eyes, but that her hair looks so wild because she has been out in the rain.

"I mean, I know I have called," she stumbles, as if following my thoughts, and I'm sure she is. If anyone could ever follow my thoughts, it was her. "But I couldn't..." She looks away, giving my hand a squeeze before releasing it to wipe the unshed tears from her lower lashes. "You were ill. So very ill. And your eyes... you were not there in them. You weren't there. So it's so very good to see you, Draven."

I've seen sick people before. I'm glad that she made the choice not to see me like that. I am glad that she protected herself.

She helps me drink from a cup and I surprise her by taking it from her hand and doing it myself. For some time, we sit in the familiar quietness that I now realize was always a comfort to us both. The rain patters on the roof and drips steadily off of it and down my window. The sound is soothing and welcomed, for with water is life.

I clear my throat and do something that I haven't done for a very long time. I try to speak. My voice is grating at first. So grating that I'm surprised she doesn't cringe, but Willow merely listens with a soft, warm smile in her eyes, as she always has.

"Thank you... for..." I pause and wince as I clear my throat again. "For making me smell like a roast chicken. I'm sure it is an improvement."

Her eyes search mine with a hint of alarm as she seems to fret that my mind has been damaged. Maybe it has. Then she twists behind her to look at the mortar and pestle coated in mashed thyme. When she returns her gaze to me, she lets out an odd puff of air. Then another. A giggle.

I smile. Her giggle turns into a laugh and a tickle rises in my chest as my own chuckle builds. Willow leans forward, her hair falling over her shoulders as she laughs all the harder. My pathetic chortle sounds more like a pair of bellows with a hole in them, but it's the best medicine I have had yet.

# Chapter Thirteen

W ithin days, I'm walking. I have to hold onto things at first and am forced to stick to laps inside my cabin, but I yearn for the outside. Willow tells me there are bees. Flies. Grass and blossoms and leaves. My heart aches so terribly to hear the rustle of leaves again that I sometimes shed tears.

My mind is put at ease to learn that Willow first came to heal me in her nightgown. A white dress. My Watcher is gone. Victoria has left. I need not fret.

On one of my rounds around the room I pause to rest by the baskets of blankets and tools that aren't ours. I wonder if we're meant to be storing them for people with leaky roofs. It takes some effort, but I manage to ease myself down into a sit beside them. I rifle through the rabbit pelts, some of which have seen better days and are already shedding, and discover a carving. I'm about to keep digging when I recognize what it is.

A falcon. Lady. Why would someone have carved my bird?

My mother enters, carrying a bucket from the well. She looks for me at my bed then her spine sags with relief when she finds me on the floor.

"What on earth are you doing?"

I hold up the falcon in question. Her expression softens. She moves over to the kitchen table, setting down the pail of water.

I haven't spoken to her since I began recovering my strength. She doesn't know that I speak with Willow so she doesn't know the difference. I don't know why I can't bring myself to make the effort for her, but I know it has something to do with the softness of Tristan's eyes.

"They are gifts," she explains. "Tokens for the man who brought our village justice. A sign of appreciation."

As I run my thumb over the falcon, I wonder who could have carved it. The likeness is a good one. I focus on that little mystery rather than letting my mind meander in the knowledge that Morrot is trying to thank me for killing Elias. My stomach sours a bit anyway.

When at last I am well enough to leave the cabin, Willow holds my arm to keep me steady. My mother opens the door and I step outside. The sunlight is gentle and brilliant and the first impression I have is of the colors blue and green. Blue in the sky. And green... there is grass growing against the side of our house. Little plants all over the yard. The pines I used to climb as a boy are largely orange and bare, but ferns have sprung up beneath them. So very many ferns. And deeper in the forest, I can glimpse new leaves. Other pines have survived. Oaks. Cedar.

When a little bird begins his melodious, ululating song, something deep inside me is pushed over the edge. Suddenly I'm falling, but not because I have lost my balance. Willow eases down with me, holing out a hand to stop my mother from rushing to my side as I sink onto my knees. My chest is quaking and my breaths are shaking.

I can feel the cold graininess of the soil pinching my knees through my trousers. Smell the sweetness of the moist earth. The light spreads over my skin that drinks it in with a hunger for its teasing warmth that I have never before felt.

Uncontrollable tears fall from my eyes. Willow wraps an arm around my waist to support me as I weep, rubbing my back with the other. I lie down so that I can feel the earth against my body. The sprigs of seedlings against my cheek that has become bearded in my illness. The songbird continues to chortle and I have never heard a more glorious sound.

It's the first time in my life that I have ever shed tears of joy.

Joy. I feel so much joy that I am drowning in it.

As the weeks pass, I feel as if I'm healing with the world. There is a pine sapling growing just within the cleared space of our yard. It grows taller and adds more needles just as I am able to walk around for longer and grow thicker. I'm constantly amazed by how resilient our land has proved to be. It makes me smile more times in a day than I ever thought possible. There are already pastures of cattle and sheep. The latest trading excursion brought a pregnant sow from the south, so now the squealing of piglets can be heard every now and then on the breeze.

I spend my days going for walks around our property and into the recovering woods. I nap in the sunlight and have named all of our hens. Willow often comes by with Jasper who likes to make fun of my beard. I have left it for now because I know it helps hide my gaunt cheeks and I don't want my mother or anyone else to have to face any reminders of loss or starvation. The graveyard is full of young headstones.

The wound on my neck has closed, though it still occasionally pains me. I expect it always will. I don't mind the scar, wretched as it is right now. I ought to have some record of where I have been.

One afternoon, Willow and Jasper wake me up from a dreamless slumber in a sunny patch of grass a few yards into the forest. They have a basket with them and inside is something I can hardly fathom. Bread, cheese and jam. Blackberry jam. I don't ask where it came from. It takes all of my willpower already to keep from eating the entire basket, much less to take the time to slice the white cheese and place it on the bread before smothering it in jam. I savor each and every mouthful.

In the darkness, I had forgotten the pleasure of eating.

"Ned says he saw that cat again, Lil," Jasper announces, sucking jam off of his thumb.

"I hope this isn't another of Ned's tales," Willow replies. She has finished her meal and is leaning back on her elbows, her eyes closed as she enjoys the sun on her face. Her freckles are darker now, her skin a healthy pink. No longer pale and sallow. She's filling out, as well. And Jasper no longer looks frail. It's such a relief to not have to worry about his impending death.

"What cat?" I ask around a mouthful.

Willow cracks open an eye to look at me, and in the light it looks like the green of the newest leaf. "Ned thinks someone's cat survived the darkness."

"He didn't say that," Jasper swiftly corrects, his tone both defensive and argumentative. The light likewise catches in his pale eyes, making him sneeze. It's an odd reflex that happens to him multiple times a day. "He only said that he has seen it twice."

"And how old is Ned again? Three?" I ask as I swallow.

"*Five*," Jasper replies.

"Of course," Willow giggles.

Jasper snatches up a clump of grass and tosses it at her which makes her laugh again.

"A five year old still has eyes," the boy contends.

"I should hope," I tease, closing my eyes and leaning my head back like Willow. My hair is longer now than I would have normally kept it. Long enough to get tangled if I don't brush it, and I have never liked brushes. While it will never get as golden as Willow's, the sun is bringing out honeyed streaks in the blonde that distract my peripheral vision when the loose strands flutter near my face.

Indignant, Jasper rises. "May I please go feed the hens?"

"You may."

He scampers off, calling for my mother who will help him reach the grain which is safely secured in a barrel. Once his voice is distant, Willow speaks.

"They ask for you, you know."

I crack open an eye to study her face. She shifts to sit cross-legged, facing me. She's in a green calico dress with a pink pinafore that hasn't fit her for some time for it was too baggy on her form. It reminds me of how she used to dress when she was little. She reads the question in my eyes.

"Everyone. Everyone who knows that I've been visiting with you," she explains. "They all want to know how you are getting on and when you'll be well enough to... well. To be seen."

I look away from her and distract myself by watching a beetle trying to navigate a blade of grass, not seeming to understand that its own weight is making the blade bend. It has been a month now since the day I awoke to Cavan in my house, offering me honeyed water. Maybe a little more.

Bending another blade of grass towards the beetle, I make a ramp for it to walk down. After bumbling for a few more seconds, it seems to notice what I have done and scurries downwards towards the soil. I can feel Willow's eyes watching me.

By the time I calm my thoughts enough to meet her gaze, she has already looked away. She's gazing downward, unfocused, a slight pinch in her features. I know the look well by now. Something has reminded her of him. She's feeling both her pain and her love for Tristan at the same time.

I have never told her about my Watcher. About what happened with Victoria at the house. To do so would not only salt Willow's wounds, but would add more confusion between us when there is enough already. Even now when I can think clearly, I have never been able to puzzle out why Victoria chose me. Perhaps because Willow is a Listener and she knew that I was close to Willow. That she could use me as a pawn to wound the other girl. While that makes sense with everything Willow has told me about Victoria, something is missing. After all, Victoria's death is what started the darkness, but I saw her in the woods even as a child. Which would mean that I saw her while she was alive.

If that is so, then she was much older than Tristan when she died, for she was an adult eighteen years ago when I was just a boy. It's these troublesome details that keep me from telling Willow, for we have the sunlight and our lives, and if we have overlooked a strand of this web we were both caught in, then perhaps the Bringer of Darkness is not gone, after all. That is a complication neither of us can face quite yet. But she deserves to know that death didn't end Tristan.

"Willow..." I start. The chickens cluck in the distance as they see Jasper approaching with their feed. Their feet pitter patter on the ground as they run to him. "Do you ever... do you hear him?"

She won't look at me now and I'm left with her profile. Her loose hair flutters slightly in the gentle breeze. Her features grow even tighter. She hesitates then swallows with some effort.

"No," she whispers at last.

"Do you ever see him?"

After a moment, she turns to fix me with a questioning look. I pretend not to notice the way her eyes and nose are shimmering with the telltale signs of fighting back tears. I always pretend not to notice.

"You know I can't," she whispers, and somehow the act of speaking loosens her tears. She wipes at them immediately. As if ashamed. I never want her to feel shame.

I nod. Normally I would give her a moment to compose herself, but today I can't. Not when I know she's trying to bury him for my sake. As if I'm the one aggrieved.

"I saw him," I say, more suddenly than I had planned. Her watery eyes latch onto mine with such intensity that it takes me a moment before I can continue, for my breathing hitches. "When I was sick, I was... dying. I was able to sit with him. Speak with him. Visit with him."

Two tears fall at the same time, jetting down her cheeks and she absently wipes at them. "What did he say? How was he? Is he frightened?"

I shake my head. "No, no nothing like that. He was very... charming."

She lets out a happy puff of air that is a relative of a laugh as a little smile forms on her lips. "I wish you could have known him."

"So do I."

A line forms between her brows. "Why did he come to you?"

I suck in a deep breath and hold it, studying the soil beneath the grass, looking for the beetle. Instead, I see ants, waving their antennae as they navigate. "I don't know," I reply as honestly as I can, for I've been trying to answer that question myself ever since I have had the space in my mind to do so.

I feel Willow nod beside me. She sniffles again as she looks out to the decaying and healing trees around us. "What did he say?"

"He wanted to... explain things. To me."

I study her profile. The fresh tears are gone but their light shadow remains beneath her eyelids, glistening. She sniffles again but her breathing is calmer. When the sunlight also catches on the shimmer beneath her nose, I'm filled with such admiration for her bravery that it nearly sends my bee-letters into the wind.

May I find such courage.

"Victoria?" she asks with croaking throat.

"And Elias. And..." I take a small breath. For half a heartbeat I'm again trying to distract myself by looking for the beetle but wrench my eyes back to her profile. "And you."

She closes her eyes. For a moment, her expression is serene and I wonder if she can feel him in the breeze. Everything about her right now confirms what I've had to learn again and again: that however long our friendship, however deep our roots within each other, we have never loved. I know this for certain because I'm looking at the face of love right now, even with one half of it missing.

Before I know it, my throat is tightening. I try to swallow past the feeling and relax my muscles, but it has started a process I can't stop. I know what is coming even if I can't understand any of it.

Willow gasps, screwing her eyes shut, her face twisted with such pain. "I miss him so much," she squeaks. Her strong form is suddenly bent. Broken.

I close the gap between us. Pull her to my side. I hold her and she slumps against me like a sigh. Jasper has always been with us before, ever since I have been well. We have never been afforded this moment that so needed to break over the pair of us.

"I miss him so much," she repeats in a whine against my tunic.

"I know, Willow," I try to soothe, but my own tears are straining my throat and eyes. "And he did not want to leave you."

I feel in the tension of her muscles the need to say that he never left at all. That he was taken. But that would bring to life the reason I have yet to speak to my mother. That would release the bolt she fired at Tristan all over again. So Willow doesn't say anything. Only weeps.

"You saved him," I gasp, and she quiets for a moment when she hears the tears in my voice, as well. "You saved him."

I cannot tell her that I begged him to stay. To live with her in whispers. I cannot tell her that he made a choice to leave. So instead, we cling to each other's bony ribcages and tousled hair, weeping for Tristan. For Lady. For my father and Scarlet. For the darkness and the hunger and the fear. We weep for Jasper's shortness and our parents' age. We weep for my illness and my recovery. We weep for each other.

After some time, I hear my mother in the distance, calling Jasper to her because he's probably watching us with worry. I don't mind. We have all hidden our bruises for far too long. It's not such a terrible thing to grieve. In fact, once we manage to stop weeping and are both a pile of disheveled hiccoughs, I haven't felt such relief in ages.

With a shuddering breath I collapse onto my back. I've been upright for too long. Willow gently lies down beside me, resting her head on my shoulder and an arm on my chest. I place a hand on her arm and gently stroke its length. It's some time before my lazy hand runs all the way to hers and I make a discovery. Her palm is on my left breast. She is feeling the beating of my heart.

I shift to look at her when I realize this and she gazes at me with the most terrible, bloodshot eyes. But they are dry. Clear. Clearer than they have been since she volunteered as a sacrifice. A veil had lain between us, even when we couldn't notice it. A tense and burned, mildewing thing. An ugliness birthed from her love for another man. From Victoria's manipulation. From being afraid that I was only going to die and leave her like Scarlet and Tristan. The veil is gone now. Dissolved by our tears and the simple honesty of our hearts.

Willow will always love Tristan, and I will always regret that he is no longer here for her. We have forever shifted the way that we fit or don't fit together. There are no more innocent gifts of braided grass bracelets. I will adore Willow, as I always have done, but without the delusion that she's anything more than a steadfast friend. We love each other, yes. But there are many kinds of love. I'll never be able to shake the hope I once kindled with her, but even now, I couldn't tell you what it was that I hoped for. Just something... more. But there's no greater gift than a true friend, and Willow is my friend.

Somehow, I sense her unraveling similar thoughts as she looks into my eyes and notices the stillness of my hand on her arm. Both are resting over my heart. Then her eyes shy away from mine and she scoots her body closer to me, resting her forehead against my neck. We lie like this for some time, absorbing the last light of the grove as the sun shifts its angle. Just when I wonder if she has fallen asleep, she speaks.

"You really need to shave."

Though a laugh bubbles up in my chest, I let it out by rubbing my hairy chin on the portion of her forehead that I can reach. Willow squawks and leans away with a giggle and shove.

# Chapter Fourteen

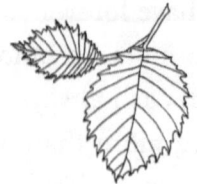

Several days later, I do shave. I shave and comb and braid my hair. More offerings have been left on our door. They remind me of the food and tokens once given to Elias and I want nothing to do with him, even if I am his killer. I don my freshly washed green tunic over my leather trousers and hook my crossbow onto my belt. Collecting the latest two baskets full of apples and meats and cheeses that I desperately want to eat, I step out of the house. My mother is still asleep and doesn't even notice that I have left.

The walk to the village feels much longer than it ever has before. I must stop several times to catch my breath. I'm thankful that the baskets were not more laden, for their few pounds seem to increase in weight every few yards. I'm not nearly as recovered as I had thought. My mother warned me that it would take months, not weeks, but I'd been determined to prove her wrong.

I pass the first few houses, delighted to see laundry drying on lines in the yards. Hens in coops. In the distance, sheep bleat in pastures. Morrot is still healing yet feels more alive than I had ever hoped it could be again. Despite the tiredness lingering in my body, I feel invigorated by the life around me and can't help but smile.

A woman is outside of her house, hanging up large strips of dripping purple fabric that drizzle equally purple water. Dye. Of course. She's the woman who used to spin and dye yarn. She stares at me as I pass. She's the woman who once slapped me when I bought yarn for my mother as a child.

I look away as soon as her gaze meets mine. Under the weight of her eyes I know how loosely my clothes hang on my broad-shouldered frame. How unsightly the scar on my neck is. How small I really am inside.

I recall the weight of the yarn in my basket. How kind I thought her face looked as she smiled down at me. I had smiled back.

"Aren't you going to say 'thank you'?" she had asked.

All it ever took back then was a question from a stranger to silence me. My bees took flight. I couldn't speak. I couldn't even smile anymore.

"Go on, now, I can't hear you," she had insisted.

I couldn't tell her that I wasn't going to say the words that I felt. The yarn was beautiful. Dark green. My mother later used it to make my cowl. But this woman couldn't understand any of that because my words were gone. I shook my head. The slap that followed was as abrupt and stinging as it was unexpected. I ran away as swiftly as I could. I have felt the echo of its ache every time she has looked at me since. My cheeks burn and I focus on the path ahead, ignoring her.

Bethany. Her name is Bethany. I have pretended not to know it for a decade.

Ethel's kids are outside of their house, playing with a hound puppy as I pass by. The dog must have come from a trade in the south. The youngest of the boys tries to hold the dog in his arms as they watch me pass. After having just seen Bethany, I'm surprised that I can offer them a smile.

I shift the baskets in my arms, ignoring the sweat that's now slipping down my hairline and collecting on my chest and back. I really am far too weak to have attempted this but I didn't know what else to do. I cannot keep all of these gifts and I don't deserve any of them. Not for killing a man. Though it had to be done, it was still murder.

There is another pair of eyes on me. A woman shaking out a rug on her doorstep. Then another: a young husband helping his emaciated wife walk around the cow pen outside their house.

"Mama!" Ethel's boy without the puppy calls, darting back inside. "Mama, Draven's here!"

A voice from another house answers. Before I have any real notion of what's happening, people are pausing in their work and stepping out of their homes to look at me. If my cheeks were flushed from the weight of the baskets, they are even darker now.

My step slows as I pass the tongs and anvil that used to be Aiken's workstation. The blacksmith is there now, fiddling with what he has left. Upon the anvil rests the hammer. I can't take my eyes off of it as I pass, because now everyone is looking at me. The heat spreads to the back of my neck.

This was a mistake. A mistake.

When I spot old Andrew watching me from the shade by the well, I pick up my pace. I don't have words for all of these people. Only for one family. So I pretend that I don't hear anyone calling my name. Asking how I am. I pretend that I am not me at all.

I knock on Willow's door. When her mother answers, I don't wait to be invited in but rather shove through.

"Drave—" she begins but cuts herself off when I slide in and set down my baskets.

"For you," I pant, looking at the ground. I have seen too many faces. Read too many confusing expressions. I don't know what it all means and I'm too tired to try.

"More?" she asks.

My curiosity gets the better of me. My eyes travel. Their house also has baskets. One with fruits and vegetables and another with fabrics.

"Gifts," Cavan explains as he rises from his place by the fire where he is roasting a rabbit on a spit, "for the Destroyer of Darkness."

"Willow," I say.

"Yes," her mother answers.

"She's with Jasper," her father continues. "Foraging."

I nod, though the action is stiff. I feel the two of them exchanging a look behind my back.

"We cannot possibly keep up with what our neighbors have given us," her mother continues. "You and Gwen need the food. We have enough."

Though she rests her hand on my arm, I still can't bring myself to lift my eyes from the baskets of provisions on their floor.

"We have enough," she softly repeats.

That's all I need to hear and the air is too close in here. Clammy. I grab my baskets and step back outside. It isn't much better. I had forgotten what heat feels like. True heat.

Willow doesn't need the food and I cannot accept gifts for a murderer. I spot Andrew still in the shade by the well and make my way over to him as quickly as I can. He's the one who found my father's necklace in Elias' library. Who got me the honey that helped save my life. Who everyone laughed at as the village drunk.

Andrew watches me from beneath his scraggly grey eyebrows as I approach. Kneeling beside him, I break off some cheese and bread from my basket and press the food into his palm. The old man looks from the sustenance in his hand then up to my face, his bearded chin quaking. Remembering the fruit, I also give him an apple. But there is plenty more. Plenty.

Ethel's boys are nearby, having tailed me with their hound puppy on a rope. Their tunics hang off of their bodies, as well.

"Come here," I command. They freeze, as if in shock that I have spoken. "Boys, come."

They do so, and as they approach, I realize that much like Jasper, they are smaller than they ought to be at thirteen and ten.

"For you," I say, giving them each an apple and some cheese.

"Thank you," the older breathes. "Thank you so much."

I nod then notice the young couple outside of their house by the cow paddock. They don't yet have a heifer. Both are leaning against the fence rails to catch their breath so I make my way over and hand them the basket with the bread and cheese. The wife immediately holds out her hands as if to refuse so I snatch her outstretched wrist and force her to hold the basket.

I still have the fruit, and by now there are even more people outside and watching than there were before. So I hand out apples, realizing for the first time that it must be near autumn for them to be so plentiful, even if it only feels like spring in our valley. Children surround me with a chorus of thanks as I press fruit into dirty little hands.

The basket is nearly empty when something is dropped inside. A ball of dark green yarn. It's the first thing to make me look up since I began handing out the fruit. Bethany is standing before me, her once portly frame diminished, her cheeks sagging. I'm now taller than her but still, I want to look away. Want to. But I don't. I force myself to meet her pale eyes. There's a hint of sorrow in them as she sets another ball of dark yarn in my basket.

The sight of the moth eaten wool makes the memory of the pain in my cheek flare at the same time that I feel a tightness in my throat. She is walking away before I can sort out my thoughts. I cannot speak, so I drag a step forward. The sound of my boot on the gravel makes her look over her shoulder. I hold out my last apple. When she takes it, I can see her lower jaw tremble.

"Thank you," she croaks.

I nod with the smallest smile. It's all I can do.

Then I hurry home.

My mother is adding a potato that she has carefully sliced to the soup in the cauldron over the flames. I fling the door shut behind me and immediately slump into a chair on the table, staring at the moisture left on the knife from slicing the vegetable. My sweat has cooled and I should be chilled but instead I'm warm all over from the memory of all of those eyes watching me. Asking of me.

"Where is the bread, Draven?" my mother asks.

I close my eyes and clasp my hands together, hugging them in towards my chest.

"And the cheese? The apples?" When I don't reply, she lets the wooden stirring spoon clatter against the side of the pot and steps over to me. "Draven, where is our food?"

"It was not ours," I grind out, easing my eyes open the slightest bit. Even through my lashes, I can see her stiffen at my voice. "It was never ours."

"Don't be foolish," she softly reprimands, all accusation gone.

I pivot to face her. "We are not the only ones who need to eat."

She slowly shakes her head, drying off a hand on her stained apron over her dress. In the filtered light that shadows all of the lines on her face, I realize that I don't have any real idea of how old my mother is.

"After each trading mission, there is a vote because there is never enough food to go around equally. And after each trading mission, the vote has been to give the bulk of the goods to Willow's family, for breaking the darkness, and to us, for—"

"For killing." I meet her gaze as her mouth grows tight. "For murder."

She takes a moment, her thin lips growing even more wane before she releases the corner of her apron that she was using to dry her hand. "For justice."

I shake my head and look away. The sudden longing to be in my grassy patch among the dead pines strikes me, along with the disappointment of knowing that at this time of day, the sunlight will have already moved on and I will be in the shade. My body is too tired to travel farther than that. There is no escaping this moment. I dig my fingers into the hair around my braid, loosening it.

"My son," my mother begins, her voice closer to me than it was before. "You ended the life of a corrupt, evil man. Not because you wanted him dead, but because you wanted him stopped."

"I wanted him dead," I flatly reply.

She doesn't know how to respond to that. The fire murmurs quietly. The soup in the pot lets out soft gurgles as it boils. Outside, a crow is calling.

"So did I," she softly says. "So did Cavan and his family. So did dozens of others. We all must pay for our crimes."

I turn my head to look at her, my loosed strands of yellow hair falling in my face. "And so must I."

"They bring our household gifts to thank us," she explains in a rush, sliding into the chair beside mine and resting a hand on the back of my shoulder. "To thank *you*. To ensure that you heal and thrive, Draven. No one faults you for taking the life of a man who has already taken so much from all of us."

"Yes. *A man*. He was still a man. Not an animal. And I ended him like one."

"You were merely an instrument of our will," she insists, giving my shoulder a light squeeze. "Don't forget that his actions caused the darkness. He does not only have Lucian and Scarlet's blood on his hands, but that of Aiken and everyone else who has succumbed to hunger or disease these past years. Willow may have broken the darkness, but you destroyed our fear. Had Elias been allowed to live, he would still be in power now, and who knows what terrible deeds he would bring about."

My throat is tight and I wait for my eyes to water with tears. They don't. Instead, I meet her gaze. "Oh, Mother. You also killed a man."

Her hand slowly recoils from my shoulder, her eyes searching mine. I wait for the curtain to fall over them as it has so often after father died. For her to retreat into herself. Instead, she holds my gaze and keeps her chin steady. "And I shall have to live with that mistake until the end of my days, and mayhap even longer."

When her fingertips again find my shoulder, I rest my hand on top of hers.

I was right about it being near autumn. As my endurance returns I take to longer meanders through the forests. Some of the trees that I had thought were dead aren't dead at all. A gentle nick in their bark reveals moist green and yellow wood. They are simply hibernating as they have all through the darkness, waiting for the true spring. I remind myself not to wish for time to go by faster, no matter how I long to see more leaves. It's enough to have sunlight. It's enough to be.

One chilly morning while my mother sleeps, I'm stoking the fire when I hear a light thump out the door. Crossing the room, I open the door to find another basket of bread and cheese placed just outside. A woman in a headscarf is walking away.

This must end.

Picking up the basket, I trot over to her and hold it out, silently asking her to take it back. When her face turns to mine, I stop walking.

"Megan."

She likewise halts at the sound of her name. Her face is still thin but looks far less skeletal than it did during the darkness. She smiles, the tip of her nose pink from the brisk air, her cheeks flushed from the walk. After all, she and I live on the opposite fringes of the village. A small laugh escapes and her cheeks color even more. She looks away bashfully.

"I have just... I am not accustomed to hearing you actually speak my name."

The revelation makes heat creep up the back of my neck, as well. I know I'm hunching but I can't stop.

"Sorry," I whisper.

For a moment, she tugs on the corner of her dark blue scarf to hide her smile, then seems to think better of it and straightens to meet my gaze once more. Her expression becomes sincere. "Are you going to give away my bread again?"

I arch a brow as I glance down at the perfect loaf.

"You certainly could not have thought that it was my—"

She cuts herself off and looks away. There is a sternness in her jaw that I have never seen before. It's the first reminder I have ever had that she is Bram's daughter. Bram the miller. Bram the teller. The betrayer.

"I didn't know," she continues, a few strands of her red hair escaping her cowl and fluttering across her forehead in the light breeze. Every freckle on her face seems to stand out in the overcast light, matching her hair. I know they will give her a youthful appearance long after her hair begins to grey. When her words take no root in my thoughts, she repeats them. "Draven, I swear, I didn't know."

I nod. Somehow, I have always known this. Been able to separate her father's actions from hers. Perhaps if her father's actions had been successful I would feel differently. If Elias were still alive and in power, then maybe I would—no. Because if Elias were still alive and in power, then I would be dead.

"Elias made promises to him," she continues. There's moisture in her eyes, either from tears or the breeze. "That our family would be safe from the lottery. I cannot forgive him for what he has done, for what almost happened to you, but he was... he..."

"He was desperate," I softly finish for her, recalling Cavan's words to my mother.

Megan's eyes are fixed on mine, her lips parted slightly as if in surprise over my acceptance.

"What's done is done." I once again hold the basket out to her. "If we dwell on such things then the darkness will never truly lift."

The tears in her eyes pool until she blinks them away. Her gaze wanders down to my hands. She reaches out her own pale fingers and lightly traces them over the back of my hand where one of my white scars from Lady's talons is peeking out from under the tunic sleeve. Her cold fingertips slide down to the basket. She takes a hold of the handle then pushes it back towards me.

"Keep it." There is a plea in her eyes that's stronger than that in her voice. "Please. Just this once."

Though it makes me uncomfortable to do so with the memory of Ethel's boys and the rest of the children, I nod. It has never been about me wanting the food. I have always wanted it. I'm terribly hungry nearly all the time. But so is everyone else. I'm no different from the rest of them. But I will take a basket just this once because it's what Megan needs to let go of her father's actions.

I shift my grip so that the weight of the handle slides into my palm and Megan offers me a smile of thanks.

"I hope I will see you soon," she says.

The word "likewise" comes out of my mouth before I'm even aware that I'm forming the sounds. With another little smile, she steps away from me, tightening the scarf around her head with one hand as it billows slightly in the breeze of her brisk pace.

Not wanting to stare at her slender form, I step back into the house. Once inside, I pick up the bread. It's dense and round. I inhale its sweet scent, noticing that it's still warm in the center. Still warm.

# Chapter Fifteen

Megan isn't the only one who left offerings of food. The next evening that the trading party returns with wagons and mules laden with dried goods, I want to make sure that I'm present. If there is to be a vote, then I want to witness it. To tell everyone that what they have been doing is not unappreciated but that it is unfair.

I had hoped that the walk into town would be enough to calm my bee-letters, but they hum with nervous tension all the same. As such, it's a relief when Willow meets me by the well.

She speaks for us both and bids the villagers to divide up the goods evenly. Some protest, used to the way Elias was supported by Morrot. The rest go along with our will. After all, if autumn is here, then winter is coming and we must be prepared to face it.

When next I see Megan, it's a warmer day but she's still in a head-scarf. When I recall her thinning hair, I know why.

We are on a walk down the path from my house to the village. Our bodies aren't touching but there are only a few inches between us. When she pauses to watch the cat that has now become legendary thanks to Ned and his stories, I rest my hand on her head. It's enough to fully direct her attention to me and she fixes me with her questioning brown eyes.

Giving her scarf a gentle tug, I wait to see if she'll reach up to stay my hand, but she doesn't. I pull off her headscarf and she casts her eyes away. Her hair is growing back in downy little tufts where there used to be bald patches. Though she still has chunks of longer strands, they are thinner than they were in the darkness. Her head looks like a poorly weeded garden and she seems to know it. After all, she was one of the few households with a mirror.

When she still won't meet my gaze after several moments, I curl my forefinger and rest it beneath her chin. She looks at me and I arch a brow.

"It is still have the prettiest hair color of anyone," I assure.

A crooked smile twists her pink lips and she yanks the scarf off of her neck. "I'm the only girl with this hair color."

I offer her a small shrug with my smile and she appraises me for a moment. It's as if I can see the confidence of my compliment hopping from freckle to freckle.

She doesn't put the scarf on her head for the rest of the walk back to her house, even when we pass through the heart of the village. Instead, she balls it up and swings it around absently and meets the gaze of anyone who dares stare at her. I like her defiance. It reminds me to hold my shoulders back and my head high because I am watched now more than ever before.

Watched. Only not by my Watcher. Those days ended with Victoria. I try to keep such thoughts far from my mind but they are hard to keep at bay late at night when the snow falls and the wind whistles through the roof. When the delights of green leaves and warm winds have faded. I lie awake remembering the strangeness of the house in the woods. The pressure of Victoria's ghastly presence, even when she was just a patch of ominous dark in the kitchen. The way her touch has left me feeling as if no one else should ever touch me again. Unclean.

I fret that all the sunlight in the world won't be able to burn away her stain.

Yes, late at night, I marvel at all I have seen. I have been kissed by a corpse. Bitten by a madwoman. Spoken with a dead man. Nothing in my life leading up to the darkness had ever made me believe that such abominations could be possible. Not even Willow being a Listener.

"No, not nothing," a voice in the back of my mind slithers. "You heard the trees once, boy. The taunting of the alders by the river..."

"No," I whisper.

I could not have heard the trees. I could not have heard anything but my own thoughts. I was only a child then. So young. It was all in my head. All in my head.

I screw my eyes shut and roll over, yanking a quilt over my head to try to block out the wailing of the wind. Just when my mind starts to wander to Willow, wondering if she is also asleep beside Jasper, I stop myself. I have to do that a lot these days. I never noticed how deeply she was rooted in me until I began trying to cut off any buds of hope before they bloomed.

I spend my snowy days with Cavan and Jasper in the woods, helping him teach the boy how to hunt. There isn't much game this season. Mostly rodents and birds, lots of birds, but I try not to worry. The larger prey will return with the grass and the green. Jasper does his best to learn but it's difficult for him to focus for very long.

A few weeks in, I shift tactics and offer to teach him how to fish. We bring my father's net to the river. Without thinking, I guide Jasper to the spot where we used to fish when I was small. The spot where I had thought I could hear the trees. While Jasper inspects the water, I eye the dormant branches of the alders. The wind cuts gently through them, only making a few twigs twitch. Standing beneath them, I close my eyes. I listen.

The wind. I listen.

A hiss. I listen.

A voice.

"Draven?"

My heart leaps into my throat. I open my eyes. The skeletal fingers of the alders reach for the sky, barren.

"Drave?"

Jasper. Only he calls me that, and even then it's a new nickname.

I turn around to find the boy watching me curiously, holding the fishing net. With a soft clearing of my throat, I step over to him, tugging on my cowl as it itches the scar on my neck.

"What tracks did you see?" I ask.

Jasper grins. "There was a deer."

The news is enough to make me stop in my tracks. I smile. "Show me."

A few weeks later, Jasper has caught two fish and a hare. I come over to eat with his family on the night of each catch, even if there is only a mouthful of meat for each person. Willow is doing better. She smiles more readily and doesn't always have to fight back tears. At the dinner table, she laughs at Jasper as he imitates one of the growing piglets, telling a story about how the poor creature escaped and it took ten people to catch it and put it back in the pen with its mother.

Midwinter arrives within days. There are bonfires lining the streets of town. It's our first occasion to drink the cider that has been brewing since autumn. Some people have even baked cakes for each other like we did in the old days before there was even a shadow in the sky. Young Felicity is playing the fiddle once more, as she did at Megan's birthday celebration, but this time she is accompanied by several adults also making music.

As I walk down the main street, I'm tempted to hide under the hood of my cowl but I resist the urge. There are expectations on me now and I'm better at meeting them than I was a few months ago. I keep my shoulders back and my head high and meet the gaze of every onlooker I pass. I have never been greeted by more smiles in my life. The sensation of knowing so many wish me well is ticklish: both pleasant and uncomfortable.

My mother is wrapped in a cloak, sipping cider and swaying to the music, chatting with Willow's mother by one of the bonfires in the main street. I'm happy to see her smiling and socializing. I'm happy just to see her out of the house.

Drinking alone, his arm in a sling, is Scott. From the way people spoke about him, I had assumed that his wound was mortal. When he notices my gaze, I don't look away. Instead, he does, pretending to have just noticed a stain on his tunic and plucking at it with two fingers while holding his mug. All he manages to do is spill cider all down his front. In need of spectacles, indeed.

Ethel's oldest son darts up to me, their growing hound puppy on his heels. I pause as he approaches and he hands me a smoked fish.

"Happy Midwinter," he offers before dashing off with his dog.

As if some custom was just begun, I am suddenly being approached by half a dozen well-wishers. Sven, Aiken's younger brother who is my age, gives me ten bolt shafts to make arrows. Bethany hands me a new pair of woolen trousers. Ned, the cat story-teller, gives me a strip of sinew. By the time they all wish me a happy Midwinter and disperse, my arms are laden. On the top of my odd pile is a scone.

After standing awkwardly in the middle of the street for several moments, I spot Andrew leaning against one of the barrels of cider, swilling from his cup and laughing with another reveler. Willow is just beyond him, sitting on a log beside a smaller fire on the edge of the field outside her house. I hand the scone off to Andrew as I make my way over to her.

Willow smiles up at me in greeting, her hair looking all the more golden against the red of her cloak. At first I think it's new until I realize that I've seen it before, just not in some time. It was Scarlet's. I let my weight fall onto the empty patch of log beside her rather unceremoniously, my pile of gifts bouncing in my lap.

She laughs softly. "Happy Midwinter."

With a jerk of her head towards her cabin, I see a similar pile of gifts that she has received. While it's customary to give gifts during the festivities, usually it's only to those in immediate family or close enough, not those you scarcely know.

For some while, we sit beside each other with our shoulders

almost touching, watching the revelry going on in the streets around the larger fires. My mother is still talking with Willow's. The fiddles are playing a lively tune. Jasper, Ned, and a pack of other children are playing some sort of chasing game that involves hurling little dirty snowballs at each other. The scent of the spiced cider is in the air. It's enough to tempt me even though I swore off the drink after the night I vomited it back up at Megan's party.

"Rose came to see me," Willow says so softly that it takes a heartbeat for me to return my attention to her.

Scarlet was bigger than Willow. The cloak wrapped around her is somewhat piled at her feet, making her appear smaller than she is. She blinks with hesitation I'm not used to seeing on her face.

"She... well, everyone knows now. Everyone knows that I am a Listener."

I nod pensively. For a moment I'm struck by how self-centered my thoughts have been. In my illness, I never realized just how much explaining Willow and her family would have had to do to Morrot. Tristan and his bride, the Bringer of Darkness. The house. Willow's ability. I'm so used to her gift that I sometimes forget that it's not widely known, but of course, this is a change for her.

"What did she want?" I softly ask.

Rose is around Andrew's age, only she keeps to herself. In fact, I'm surprised that she is still alive. I never saw much of her in the darkness and had assumed that she had died in her house.

Willow's jewel-like eyes reflect the firelight, like twin suns on a clear day. "To know if it is her husband who keeps moving her shawl off the hook and onto the floor every night. If it is her husband who her cat meows at and follows in the hall. If it is her husband who haunts her."

Rose is old. She must be in her seventies. I can only scarcely remember her husband. They had a child but he died in infancy. I have seen his headstone. They were childhood sweethearts. The thought of her still being so bonded with her husband, even over a decade after his death, makes me feel small and rough around the edges. Then the thought reminds me of Tristan and why he would not stay. I had thought Rose to be dead. She may as well be for all she interacts with the world.

"And is it?" I softly ask.

A small smile curls Willow's lips and she nods. "That has never happened to me before. Usually the spirits come to me. I have never been able to request one."

"He must be waiting for her."

A line forms between her brows so quickly that it makes me skip a breath. "Then why don't I ever hear Tristan?"

The pain etched on her face reminds me of the days I never want to return to. The days after Scarlet died when Willow was just a shell of herself. She remained that way for a long time, no matter how I tried to reach her. It is only now, since Tristan, that she has shown more of her fullness. It doesn't make much sense because she lost him, too, but something about how she felt for him, and him for her, opened her back up again and let her fill with light.

I part my lips, calming the buzzing of my bee-letters that are tense over what I'm about to say. I have waited long enough to tell her Tristan's decision. She has a right to—

"There you are," an alcohol and apple-tinted breath gushes from my side, startling me. I only have time to see Willow's expression crack and retreat before pivoting to look up at Megan. I had been so distracted that I never even heard her approach. She grins at me, her cheeks rosy beneath their freckles, her face regaining some of its comely fullness. Her headscarf is gone. Instead, she cropped her lingering long strands of hair to match the downy new growth.

Her hand is extended, waiting for mine. It's only then that I notice the villagers around the bonfire clapping in time to a lively tune. A reel. Dancing. People are dancing. Megan wants me to dance with her. For a moment I can't move because I need to keep speaking with Willow. Want to keep speaking with Willow. And yet I likewise need to take Megan's hand.

A weight is lifted off my lap as Willow grabs my Midwinter gifts, making the choice for me. I hold out my hand and only have a moment to cast Willow a look of gratitude before Megan tugs on our linked fingers, redirecting my attention to her in the same elegant, dark green gown that she wore at her birthday celebration.

I rise. She scampers over to one of the bonfires and her playfulness teases out a small laugh in me as I follow. A few whoops rise up when we take each other's hands and begin to dance. Whoops because people are watching. But for the first time, I don't notice them.

Megan is happy and twirling and I know that I am making her feel these wonderful things. I have never had that gift before. What a treasure. I laugh as she twirls and shakes her head, as if loosening her long locks that she no longer has. Hands clap around us. I catch a glimpse of my mother watching and keeping time with her hands, no small glint of surprise in her eyes. Megan's father pretending he doesn't notice us. Geralt sticking his fingers in his mouth to whistle.

Then the song ends and Megan is a laughing, a light mess of limbs clinging to my arms for support. She has been spinning too much. Drinking too much. I wrap my arms around her to keep her steady and she presses her forehead to my neck. The heat radiates off of her body and the sweat of her brow dampens my skin. I can feel her heart through the back of her ribcage. She is so beautifully alive.

"I have a gift for you," she says softly, twisting her neck to peer up at me. She budges to disentangle herself but I hold on a moment longer. There is something more pleasant than sunlight in giving and being wanted like this. Megan gives my torso a squeeze, as if she understands, then takes my hand and leads me out of the ring of firelight.

A rush of heat surges into my cheeks as I realize that I have no gift for her. I have no gift for anyone other than the repairs I made to the barn for my mother. In the past, I always made something for Willow, but something stopped me this year. I knew a gift from me wouldn't mean much. Just one amongst many. A drop in her well that is full of another man's brown eyes.

"Look," Megan prompts, swinging our hands once we are in the dark. She is peering upwards and I follow her gaze. The night is clear, and there are so many stars that I can easily make out the creamy, jeweled belt above us. It's been a long time since I've looked up. "Aren't they beautiful?"

"Yes," I breathe.

I gaze at them for some time. Even after I feel Megan shift her attention to gaze at me. When I don't follow the pressure of her eyes, she steps up to me. Her lips press against my jaw. My chin. My lips. I bow my head to meet her and she wraps her arms around my neck, resting them on my shoulders.

She laughs softly as I kiss her back. I don't really know what I'm doing but she keeps it up all the same, so I do, as well. It's a pleasant sensation, if gentle and teasing. Something about it seems so very odd. Perhaps it's the little smacking noises our kisses make. I don't know what to do with my hands so I rest them on her shoulders.

Megan holds her lips to mine longer and longer. It isn't just her lips. Her tongue. She uses it to tease my mouth open. To caress the tip of mine. That's when I realize there is no set of instructions for this. It isn't a dance and it isn't something I need words to for. It's trial and error and oh so very forgiving.

She lets go of me to gently hook my wrists, lowering them to her waist. My thumbs press into the green fabric of her gown as her tongue presses further into my mouth. A rush courses through my body. I know it's only natural to feel such things, that there is much about being with a woman that I have yet to experience, but I'm growing tense. My thumbs stop moving as my kisses slacken. Megan leans her weight into mine and instead of leaning into her, I back up. Only there isn't anywhere to go. After a few steps, my heels hit the wall of a house. Then my back.

"Just relax," Megan whispers.

I try. But not only are my bee-letters buzzing amok, but my heart is racing as if I were excited or terrified and I can't tell which. Closing my eyes, I mimic the movement of her tongue. I seek some pleasure or enjoyment. What little was there to begin with can no longer be found.

Relax, I remind myself. Relax, relax, relax.

Even when her hands shift so that one is cupping my cheek. Even when she ignores the fact that I'm not kissing her back anymore. Even when she trails her lips down my chin and jaw, instead.

My neck. She sucks on my neck.

Victoria.

My heart's in my throat and I push on her shoulders, shoving her mouth away from me with what would be a cry if I could find the focus to make a sound. Megan stumbles backward, and even in the shadows I can see her bewildered, panting expression. A tremble courses over my entire frame.

I can't think. I couldn't find the words to explain, even if I wasn't Draven Who Does Not Speak.

Megan's eyes dart from my face to the scar on my neck and she grows tenser and relaxes at the same time. She doesn't know what happened in the house in the woods. No one does. But the softness in her expression tells me that she understands, even if she doesn't know.

Lines form on her face, making her appear older than her years. "Draven..."

She reaches out a hand for me. When I don't move to take it, she tries to close the distance between us. My bees are a swarm. My heart hammers. I do the only thing my body is begging me to do.

I run.

Darting past Megan, I run beyond the houses, away from the music and merrymaking. I run for the darkness of the trees, my boots crunching in the snow. She doesn't call after me. She doesn't follow. I don't stop until the cold air ices my lungs with pain and I can't breathe anymore. Then I hug the trunk of a cedar, struggling to breathe. I sink onto the dead needles and vacant dirt below, encircled by a ring of snow.

There, alone in the dark and the cold, surrounded by the pines and the distant scent of Morrot's woodsmoke, I press my cheek against the bark and gag out my tears. I weep because I have just shamed myself so terribly. Because I know I have hurt Megan. Because I couldn't stop myself. Because of Victoria.

Victoria. Victoria. Victoria.

All my weight is against the tree. The beautiful tree that doesn't mind my quietness at all. The beautiful tree that used to be a place for Lady to rest. I'm not even clear on where I am in the woods, but I feel safe all the same. So I cry until I have no more tears left.

At some point, I realize that I haven't heard any laughter or voices from Morrot in some time. That I can no longer hear the violins. I'm cold and curled up on the ground. Twigs and needles stick to my cheek. I must've slept. Stiffly sitting up, I brush the debris off of my skin, my cheeks tight with dried tears. I rise and gaze down at the village. The bonfires are just embers.

My mother will be worried. I must go home.

That's when something catches my eye. A pillar of white. I twist around to face whatever it is and lose my ability to breathe. My Watcher. She is back.

# Chapter Sixteen

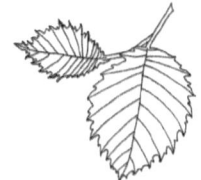

"No," I gasp on an exhale. She is still several yards off, deeper amidst the trunks, but I know it's her. Brown hair falls over her shoulders and while I can't make out her expression from this distance, I can feel her presence. It's heavy. So very heavy.

She hasn't moved on. The Bringer of Darkness is still here, taunting me.

I drop to one knee and rummage the forest floor. I find a pinecone. Rising, I hurl it at her with a scream. My Watcher steps behind a tree trunk and never comes back out. The pinecone thuds against a drift of snow.

Enough. I have had enough.

I sprint to the spot, nearly tripping as I do so, only to find the darkness of night where my Watcher had just stood. Pivoting, I peer around me, hunting for any sign of her. Every patch of snow catches my eye. White. But she is not here.

No more. No more.

I trudge back to Morrot and make my way to Willow's house. My heart is thudding and I can't stop seeing the look on Megan's face when I pushed her away. I can't control my thoughts. They are all hitched on the backs of my mad, mad bees.

I prowl around the cabin for a few minutes, calming my blood and my mind, sorting out what to do. It's late, but I don't know how late. Peering up at the stars, I realize that they have shifted quite a bit since I looked upon them with Megan. Hours have passed.

After a gentle rap on Willow's window, I wait. There's a soft rustle inside. I wait some more, then the door creaks open at the front of the house and I round the corner to greet her. She has Scarlet's cloak wrapped over her white nightgown and peers outside, having had the forethought of donning a pair of fur-lined boots. When she sees me, she slips outside and closes the door behind her.

There isn't much light, but I must look affright, for she studies me with concern for a moment before whispering, "Megan was looking for you."

I step up to her, clasping my wrists in front of my chest, having so much to say that I feel as if boulders are causing a landslide inside of me. But I cannot speak. My jaw trembles.

Willow reaches up and plucks a stray clump of needles and sap from my hair that I hadn't noticed then brushes some dirt off of my cheek.

"What happened?" she asks.

I take several steadying breaths. With each lungful, my bees calm a little more. I wouldn't feel comfortable taking such time to collect my letters with anyone other than Willow and her family. After a length of which anyone else would have given up on my response, I manage to speak.

"I saw her," I croak.

"Who?" she asks with a little shake of her head.

"Victoria."

Willow blinks, her eyes widening. "What?"

"In the woods," I explain. Maybe it's the cold, but my nose and eyes are stinging again.

"That... that shouldn't be..."

"But it is," I softly continue. "And it isn't the first time."

Willow lets out an incredulous little gasp and has to look away. After a moment, she starts walking and I follow her to the embers of the fire that had been burning near her house earlier in the night. She holds her hands over the coals then grabs a stick to stir them, tossing on a few pieces of wood.

I would tell her not to bother. That it's late and she should go back to bed. That I'm sorry for waking her at all. But I don't. Instead, I shuffle over to the log where we had sat hours before and sink down onto it. Once Willow has rekindled the fire, she does the same.

We sit in quiet for a few moments. I can hear Jasper's snoring from the house yards away. Three owls calling to each other amidst the woods across the field. The scurrying of a rat by the cider barrel.

"I have seen her for as long as I can remember."

Willow studies me with intensity as I watch the flames returning to life. Can a spirit do the same?

"You can remember a long time," Willow prompts.

I meet her gaze then. There's something about her very presence that warms my chest and calms me to the point that I can speak without trouble. Maybe it's because she's a Listener. Or maybe she is a Listener because she can make people feel so safe. Welcomed.

"I was very small when I would try to go to her in the woods. She wears a white dress. Her wedding dress, maybe. And she watches me. She is my Watcher."

A line forms between Willow's brows as her sea-green eyes search my face, and I know better than to assume that she isn't reading more information there.

"She was there that night," I continue softly, "when I thought I was tracking a deer. She stood outside of the house just before the windows lit up. She led me there so that she could..." I blink, my eyes suddenly stinging. I hope it's from the smoke. I can't shed anymore tears tonight.

"You've never told me what happened."

"You've never asked." I busy myself picking up the stick and prodding a branch to push it further into the flames.

"No, I suppose I haven't," she agrees, her voice nearly drifting away. "I have been far too selfish for that."

"You haven't been selfish."

She lets out a short, mirthless chuckle and won't meet my gaze.

"Willow, you have not been—"

"I haven't been anything," she continues with the same false jest in her tone, hesitantly looking at me again. "Not a friend to you or a sister to Jasper."

I shake my head. "You spend time with him every day."

"He would rather play with Ned who is three years younger than him because I'm just a companion. Not a playmate. Not anymore. I'm just the girl who disappeared then came back and cries all the time. The girl he has to repeat himself to because I am only ever half there. Half."

"You have suffered terribly, Willow. I can't even imagine—"

"The terror of what you went through," she cuts me off, her eyes piercing mine. Her gaze is uncomfortable and cuts past every layer of scars. Then she winces. "I never, ever wanted you to get caught up in that wretched woman's feud. I wish I had been faster. Cleverer. That I could have warned you before she—"

"I was already caught up in it," I say a little louder than her. "From the darkness and her watching me and your... your sacrifice. I was never *not* a part of it all."

Willow's eyes drift to my scar. "She almost killed you."

I suck in a breath and hold it there, making myself a little taller. "But she didn't.'

Her gaze moves back up to my eyes. "I almost lost you."

A moment passes while her words weave into my thoughts and the buzzing in my breast ceases completely. There is a pleasantness inside. A pleasantness because when bees stop flying, they can make honey.

"But you didn't," I whisper.

The golden feeling inside of me wanes when she doesn't smile. Her expression is skeptical. After a few heartbeats I have to look away because I know why. We walk in circles around each other now. Every once in a while we come together and behave as if nothing has changed. The strength of a friendship since childhood allows for that. But the rest of the time we have been ignoring the unchartered territory that now lies between us. I don't have a map and neither does she.

For some time, we gaze at the fire. This is the first time we have acknowledged the differences between us now. Knowing that she knows this puts me at some ease. Because once you get to know a thing, you can learn how to get around it. Over it. Through it.

"I think she watches me," I begin softly, "because of you. Because she knows that she can get to you through me."

Willow purses her lips, watching the flames. There's something odd in the way she is chewing her lower lip. In the way she's picking at the seam of Scarlet's cloak. As if she's trying to force my words into a pattern that they simply won't fit.

Which is when I remember what Tristan told me before I woke up.

"*A Listener can only hear the dead... A Listener cannot see spirits of the dead.*"

"I am not a Listener," I say. "I cannot hear the dead."

Willow drags a hand through the hair on her temple, peering at me with it cascading down her shoulder and I know my words have echoed her thoughts. "And yet you are seeing someone without a body."

I swallow, my throat suddenly sticky as I lean my torso in closer to her. "Victoria is... is an abomination. She has found a way to be seen, just as she clung to her corpse. It's only possible because—"

"It isn't her."

"She must have always been using sunlight to make herself—"

I cut myself off as her words finally sink in.

Willow doesn't look away. "Victoria is gone. And she died five years ago, or a little longer now. Her death began the darkness. Her spirit was in her body before that. There's no way that you could have seen her as a child."

I shake my head. The calm she has helped spread through my chest is cooling. Winter is creeping in. "Some sort of sorcery or—"

"No, Draven. The only magic in the world is inside of us. Despite what Elias said about Scarlet or anything that mad woman told you, there is no such thing as witchcraft."

"But how do you know?" I insist. "You have never even left our valley."

"Draven," she continues, far more patiently than I deserve. "It isn't her. I've shared Tristan's memories. I have seen Victoria in life. She was passionate and desperate and unhinged, but she had no charms other than her body and her... her intoxicating need for another person."

I return my attention to the small fire, my head tight.

Victoria, beautiful Victoria with the glowing skin was only ever a spirit. I have known this for some time, but somehow it was easier to let her words take hold. To believe that she was something more. That there was a power at play that I couldn't understand. A power that still clings to me. My scar itches and I gently scratch it.

"I believe you, Draven," she says with a sigh then studies my profile. "Even if I have never seen a spirit before, I believe you. And you're right. I have never been outside of this valley. How could I possibly know what is out there in the world?"

"Who is she?" I whisper. "What have I ever done to her to merit being lured into that wretched... place?"

Willow's warm hand is suddenly over my own and I close my eyes at her touch. It's so welcoming and comforting and I'm so very, very tired tonight. In my mind, I can see my Watcher in the woods near the house. She had pointed at me. Opened her maw to scream. The memory makes me hunch.

"Could I be..." I hesitate, not because my words are difficult to form, but because I simply do not know if they even exist. "Could I be a Seer?" I peer at Willow. "A person who sees the dead?"

Willow shrugs one shoulder, giving my hand a squeeze. "Have you ever seen anyone else who has passed?"

Though I think on this, sifting through memories, I know the answer is no. My gaze falls away from hers.

"It's late," she offers with another squeeze. "You need rest. I don't think Megan would appreciate it if you were to fall asleep on a log and topple into the fire," she teases as she rises.

The other girl's name sends a dart of surprise through me.

I rise, as well. Willow tugs on my hand in farewell as she starts towards her cabin and I likewise step towards the main road.

"Do you like Megan?" I ask, a little louder than I ought to be so close to Willow's house.

Her hand was already reaching for the lever but she stops in midair, studying me with an odd expression, from what I can make out in the ambient light from our little fire. "She is a... friend."

I nod then run a hand over my face. "But do you like her?"

Willow hesitates, bunching the large red cloak around her body. "I think you mean to be asking yourself that question, not me."

She doesn't await any response. Instead, she opens the door and slips inside without even a goodnight. I feel as if I have just accidentally stepped on something of hers. Maybe I have. I don't know anymore. I don't know much of anything anymore. So I go home and I sleep for as long as I possibly can.

By the following afternoon, my mother is stacking bowls loudly in an attempt to rouse me. I groan and roll over, yanking the blanket over my head. My mother probably thinks I had too much to drink and I let her. It's easier than explaining everything that I ought to be thinking about.

The Watcher. The dead. Megan.

Instead, I have a terrible ache in my chest. A terrible ache because Willow has given me hope, as ever. Hope for something more blinded me in the past. I was like Lady with her hood on, tethered. I must find a way to grow around it, like a tree around a rope or chain that has been tied there for years. I must be able to exist with the hope for her that will not die, no matter how I try to kill it, while still being able to fly free. Untethered. This ache will not go away for it's in my heart.

Eventually, I do what I think I ought to. I get up and get dressed. Though I despise the comb, I groom my hair and braid it. My mother pretends not to notice any of this. I step out of the house. There are whiskers on my jaw but I can't bring myself to shave at the moment. It would take too much time and I'm not a dandy, anyway. At least, that's what I tell myself, as if combing my hair was some sacrifice of my identity already.

I pick branches as I go. Fir and blue spruce. I arrange them in a little bouquet with some red winterberries at the base. In lieu of flowers, it's the best I can do. I don't take the main road through the village because I know I will be seen. Instead, I make my way past the back lots of the town houses, like I used to do with Jasper when we were shifting the location of the crossbows. I miss his weight on my back. I'll have to take him out again soon.

I see the wheel of Bram's mill up ahead and a flutter of nerves stirs up the bees in my breast. Breathing deeply, I try to keep them calm. After all, I need to be able to speak to apologize. After adjusting the shoulders of my cowl, I knock on the door.

Megan's mother answers. "Draven," she greets with a smile.

I incline my head. "Good afternoon. Is Megan at home?"

"No," her father announces loudly, appearing between her mother and the door. I fight the urge to take a step backwards. "Not for you, she isn't. We don't want any troublemakers around here."

"Bram," his wife attempts to protest.

"We've had enough already," he continues then jerks his head towards the village. "Now go."

I hesitate because I know Megan is home. It's too cold out for her to be anywhere else.

"Go," Bram repeats, louder.

For several heartbeats, I do nothing other than hold the gaze of the man who betrayed not only me, but those who were with me. Those who wanted to stop the loss of an innocent life. There is tension etched in Bram's eyes. Tension that tells me he is worried I'm attempting to turn his daughter into a weapon against him. Or maybe it's that she is trying to do such to me. Either way, enough is enough.

"What was done in the dark should stay in the dark," I say as I crouch to leave the bunch of greenery on the doorstep.

Bram's wife steps away but it takes him a moment to close the door. When he does, I turn away. Out of the corner of my eye, I notice a curtain shifting, as if someone else has been watching.

There's nothing else to be done for it right now, so I leave. My head feels foggy. It's difficult to hold on to much of anything for very long. I intentionally don't look at Willow's cabin as I pass.

The following morning finds me much more relaxed, for I'm where I feel at home. I'm in the woods, this time with Jasper. We are out checking his snares, making our way through the heavy snowfall of the previous night as quietly as we can. I can't help but smile once I notice that the boy's legs are longer. He may yet grow as tall as his father.

"Nothing," he sighs when he coils up a snare that has been buried with snow.

"It was a good snare," I assure him.

"I wish Lady was still here."

I sigh as I drop into a crouch beside him, scanning the top of the snow for the indentations of animal tracks. "So do I."

"She could catch anything."

Lady. Yes, yes, I need a bird. That will help me feel right again.

The snow reveals that a weasel has passed by, but little else more. I'm worried that Ethel's boys are letting their hound run wild, chasing off any nearby game. The wind gently slices through the trees around us, hissing in my ears. I used to wrap those hisses into voices, didn't I?

There's a gentle tug on the hem of my tunic. I peer at Jasper in silent question. His face is alight with excitement as he shows me with his eyes what he has seen. A pair of pheasants is scratching in the exposed dirt under a thicker patch of pines. Jasper grabs my crossbow, attempting to unhook it from my belt for me.

I motion for him to remain quiet and where he is as I raise my weapon. I can't get a clear shot of either small bird from this angle. I scan the terrain, hunting for the best route to walk to get closer without startling the birds. Knowing Jasper will stay put, I move slowly. One step, stillness, then another. It takes some time. So much time that I know Jasper is huddling under his cowl for extra warmth. But hunting isn't for the impatient.

One of the birds stills, so I freeze. The eye in the side of its head is peering at me. I hardly breathe. My heart is beating so excitedly that I worry it's making my body rock. I may be about to lose my quarry. Then the pheasant returns to its scratching. I stiffly raise my crossbow.

Jasper's energy behind me is like a push forwards that I have to ignore if I'm to make a killing shot. Holding my breath, I take aim. I'm about to press on the release. To fire my bolt. Then the wind gusts, making the trees hiss.

A woman suddenly appears at my side.

I yelp. I let loose my bolt.

Spinning to my side, I catch a glimpse of white and brown then no one is there.

"Draven," Jasper scolds.

I lose my footing and drop to one knee. The pheasants are flying. I haven't hit either of them. I know for certain now that my heart is making my body shake. The snow seeps into my trousers, chilling my knee.

Jasper's boots crunch in the snow as he trudges towards me. "Never, ever, have you missed so—"

There she is again, standing just beyond where the pheasants were. Scrambling to my knees, I hook my crossbow to my belt and give chase.

"Terribly," Jasper finishes, sounding more than a little exasperated. "Wait!"

The Watcher just stands there, her dark hair fluttering. I stumble and trudge through the snow as quickly as I can. Jasper struggles behind me. When I'm within a few yards, the woman disappears again. I don't halt until I'm at the patch of dirt where the pheasants were scratching. One of my knees is burning and I know I have twisted it in my dash but I don't care. I turn in a circle, searching for any sign of her.

"The pheasants are gone," Jasper yells, still a ways behind me. "What're you doing?"

The wind gusts again. It hisses in my ears.

*You are the rabbit's child.*

I spot her far in the distance, almost blending in with the trees. I run, pushing past my own clumsiness in the snow and Jasper's confusion.

*The acorn.*

The drift isn't as deep further into the woods. I'm able to gain speed. When she steps behind a tree and disappears, she comes out from behind another further away. Then another. She is leading me somewhere.

*And the thistle down.*

The river is rushing up ahead and to my right. We are leaving Morrot behind. Far behind.

The Watcher suddenly appears a few yards to my side, prompting me to skid to a halt. I struggle to catch my breath and to make out her features, but it's difficult when my own breathing is clouding the air in front of me.

Slower now, I approach. As ever, she lingers just out of reach then steps behind another tree.

I halt, scanning the forest for any sign of where she will step out next, but she doesn't. I keep looking. East, west, south, north. Nothing. I spend so much time watching that Jasper is able to catch up and I'm able to catch my own breath.

"Draven," he gasps when he is just a few yards off.

"Could you see her?" I ask.

"See who? The pheasant?"

"The woman," I whisper to myself.

My eyes are watering from being open so wide in the cold as I scan the trees. There's no sign of the Watcher, but I'm certain she was leading me somewhere. Shifting my focus to where she had been standing, I see only a white dusting of undisturbed snow. All the same, I make my way over.

The river is still nearby, and as I scan the naked trees above me, I realize they're alders. I am not far from where I fished with my father. Not far at all.

The wind blows through the boughs. The branches wave gently

in the wind, some making squeaking noises as they rub against each other. I step forward, craning my neck to search for anything remarkable about their make when I feel something under my boot. It's the shape of a root but it moves.

Glancing down, I kick at the snow to push the thing out of my way only to realize that it's white, as well. White, thin, and curved.

"Is that a bone?" Jasper asks as he catches up behind me.

Crouching, my heart begins to race anew as I shove aside snow with my hands. More bones. A ribcage.

"A deer?" Jasper asks.

The whole skeleton isn't here. I know it won't be. The limbs will have been carried off by coyotes and other scavengers. Ravens. Even rats. But the spine is here. The spine and—

I yank my hand back and stumble onto the seat of my trousers when I spot teeth peeking through the snow. Human teeth. I stop digging.

Jasper slowly circles around to me. He halts when he likewise spots the skull.

When I meet his gaze, he's studying me with frightened eyes.

"Who is this?" he whispers.

"A lady," is all I can gasp back. "A woman."

For amidst the bones and the snow are shreds of the yellowing, decomposing fabric of a white dress.

# Chapter Seventeen

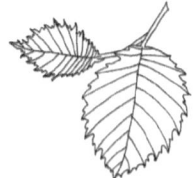

J asper races ahead of me as soon as we enter the field behind his house. He shouts for his father which I wish he wouldn't do. There really is no cause for alarm. It's not as if the bones are going anywhere.

Cavan had been on the other side of the house, chopping firewood, for he dashes around the corner with an axe in hand.

"Jasper?" he calls.

Willow appears behind him, her arms laden with split logs that she is stacking under their roof overhang. She looks from her little brother to me and I offer her a quick shake of my head to let her know that there's nothing to worry about. She dumps the firewood in the pile and dusts off her dark blue skirts.

"Someone died," Jasper gushes as he nears his family. "We found bones."

Cavan greets his son with a hand on his head then peers at me for confirmation as I near.

"Elias?" Willow asks. "Who went missing? One of the expeditions for help that never returned?"

I shake my head again as I approach the three, my boots crunching in the snow. "It was by the river."

"That's to the east," Cavan muses.

"The bones have been gnawed by mice," I explain. "Mildewed. The marrow is brittle and full of holes."

"Old," Willow concludes, a deep line between her brows.

"It's still someone dead," Jasper insists before stepping past his sister to straighten the logs she had dumped on the pile.

"At least a decade. Mayhap more," I continue.

"Curious," Cavan muses, running a gloved hand over his beard. "I cannot recall any disappearances before the darkness. Except for..." He fixes me with dark eyes.

Lucian. My father was missing for days before his body was found. I look away.

"The river is far more than a stone's throw," Cavan says. "Most of my trades are done at the pass because Elias never liked the other merchants entering Morrot."

"What if one did," Jasper says excitedly as he finishes straightening the logs. "Then Elias killed him far from the village so that no one would ever know."

We all fix the boy with what must be identical stares. He has been raised in strange times, indeed.

Jasper looks from one face above him to another. "What?" he asks.

"If you want supper then the fire needs to be hotter," Cavan says, jerking his head towards the wood.

The boy pulls a face but does as he is asked, muttering, "It's not a mad theory..." as he does so.

Once the cabin door shuts, Cavan fixes me with his pale eyes. "How old was he?"

"Fully grown."

He bites his lower lip as he nods pensively. "Very curious, indeed."

"If Tristan and Victoria made their way to our valley then perhaps others did, as well," Willow offers.

Her father hoists the axe over his shoulder with a sigh. "A decade or older?" He shakes his head the slightest bit, a skeptical gleam in his eye. "He could be anyone. And was certainly no one missed."

With that, he steps back over to the other side of the cabin to finish his chore. As I watch him leave, I feel Willow's eyes on me.

"Draven?"

I didn't realize I was biting my lower lip until I stop to meet her gaze. A moment passes between us. A moment of hesitation in which I wonder if I shouldn't say anymore. If I should keep the rest of what I saw to myself. After all, aren't I meant to be putting distance between us instead of navigating the strange territory, inching closer?

Her golden hair is tied up in a braid coiled around her head, longer than it has ever been. She hasn't cut it since Tristan died. A few stray curls flutter across her face in the breeze and I realize how much fuller her cheeks are. I can once again glimpse the girl in her who used to come visit me and Lady every day.

All the same, I am struck by something odd. Willow is not beautiful. Her face is so familiar to me that I have rarely looked upon her with the fresh eyes of a stranger, but she feels stranger now. As do I. Willow is pale and plain. She is small and curvy and only a stroke of her older sister's striking coloration. Scarlet was a beauty like Megan. Their features are the first thing a person would notice about them. But Willow... Willow is just a girl in the snow, the tip of her nose pink from the cold.

She flinches slightly under my odd gaze and looks away from me as she tucks one of her stray locks behind her ear. When I realize she is shifting her weight to leave, I speak without thought.

"It is not a man."

Her sea-green eyes dart back to mine.

"A woman," I hoarsely utter. Something shifts in her eyes and I know she understands even before I hold up the strip of yellowed, decomposing fabric from the corpse. "*The* woman."

"Your Watcher," she whispers.

The fraying fabric flutters in the breeze between us before Willow delicately takes it. She has been speaking to more villagers. Helping them find closure with those who have passed. Her ability to bid spirits of the Netherworld to step forward is growing stronger. I know what she'll say before she even speaks.

"Draven... let me help you."

No. I didn't know, after all.

"Let?" I whisper, my brows lowered.

A stern look affixes in her jaw. It's the same stubbornness she wore when she told me that she had decided to volunteer as the sacrifice. I know better than to confront it. People have had more success trying to burrow through a boulder.

I give her a small nod and just like that, the tension in her face eases. After studying the fabric for a moment, she locks eyes with me again.

"Take me there. Tonight."

"Yes," I whisper.

After supper, I say goodnight to my mother and curl up in bed. I wait until I hear her snores. I'm not a child anymore. I don't have to sneak. But she will ask questions that I would rather not answer. She will worry. So once I know my mother is asleep, I slip on my boots and cowl. I grab a bag with a rushlight, flint and steel. Hook my crossbow onto my belt.

Easing the door open, I slip outside. The moon is full so the snowscape is illuminated nearly as brilliantly as if it were day. My hand is hardly off the handle when I see a cloaked figure standing in the road. I take a step forward then pause. I was to meet Willow in the barn. Not out in the open.

The hood falls away as the figure notices me. Short hair. That is not Willow.

"Megan," I whisper as I close the distance between us. It's late and she walked a fair distance and—

"I was going to rap on your window," she whispers with a soft laugh. "How did you know I was here?"

"I didn't."

She tugs a hand out of her cloak, holding it out to me. I slip mine within hers and give it a squeeze.

"Thank you for the greenery," she offers with a small smile. Then she can't meet my eyes. "My father, he..."

"Is not you."

She looks back at me then, and in the moonlight, I am struck by her beauty. So simple. So elegant. And it is faced towards me. Megan who all the boys talked about is sneaking out of her fine home to see me. She nods, and the relief in her face tells me how long she has carried the weight of her father's choices.

"Why?" she asks softly, reaching out to rest a hand on my cheek. "Why?"

Midwinter.

"I am sorry," I whisper.

"Was it something I did?"

I shake my head, bringing up a hand to cup hers on my cheek. With a squeeze, I tug it away and kiss her knuckles.

"Not me..." she muses. "Her?"

Folding her hands in mine to warm them, a jolt goes through me as I recognize the buzzing of my bee-letters. They are readying to leave.

When her dark eyes affix on me again, they're piercing. "It was because of her, wasn't it?"

I have never told her about Victoria. She can't possibly know.

"Draven?" she urges, her voice firm.

"Megan," I softly ask, "what is it that you want from me?"

Her brows lower, creasing her forehead. She tugs her hand out of mine. "I should think that was clear."

I shake my head, remembering her party. Remembering every party. The finery of her green dress. Her elegant braids that must have taken hours. "I am not Aiken."

"I know that. Don't you think I know that?"

"Then... then why me?" I ask.

She presses her lips together with a swallow, her eyes still piercing mine before she speaks. "Because I was only ever just a girl to you. Just a girl. Not Megan the miller's daughter who liked to dance. With boys."

A corner of my mouth lifts in a soft smile that is hesitantly returned in her eyes.

She snatches up one of my limp hands. "I so admire you, Draven."

"Admire?"

The girls by the well, clapping their hands and singing their song while the boys taunted me. Hit me. One had red hair.

"Yes," she insists, squeezing my hand and leaning forward the slightest bit.

Prudence doesn't spend much time with Megan anymore, but they had both laughed as Aiken suffocated me in the mud. Mayhap there was some difference between them as they got older.

"Not only because you refused to see me as the other boys do, but because you are brave."

She delighted in telling me that Willow had left her party with Scott. Then she had danced with me. I can still hear Aiken's laugh.

"I knew you would succeed against Elias," she continues, now holding my hand in two of hers. "I knew you would one day take his place."

My gaze has drifted away, unfocused. It snaps back to hers. "Take his place?"

"Don't act so surprised. It's the will of Morrot. Someone must lead."

I have known this for months now. The necessity of a leader and the desire for me to be a part of that isn't what surprises me. Instead, it's the idea of replacing Elias. Of being even vaguely associated with him. Yes, someone must lead. And someone would seek to be the partner of that leader.

A flicker of indignation sparks to life in me but I'm quick to stamp it out. This isn't about power. I had none when she first took notice of me that afternoon when I was fourteen and elbows deep in a deer carcass. No, I had less than none.

My eyes trace the outline of her short hair. Her strong jaw. The straightness of her back. And I realize that she didn't answer my question. I had asked, why me? Her answer was herself. It is the same answer I would give if I were being honest.

She still has my hand in hers so I take a step towards her, closing the gap between us. My bee-letters are still skittish but they remain in the hive of my chest. I shake my head. "Then it's not me at all that you care for. It is yourself through me. Just as I saw myself through you."

I release her hand and step away. Her features twist with puzzlement. A dull ache settles in my chest, even though I know that I'm doing the right thing. For both of us. We have only ever been looking glasses for each other.

"I have nothing to give you," I continue, as kindly as I can. "But you were always more than Megan the miller's daughter who likes to dance with boys. And you always will be more."

Backing away, I watch her just long enough to see my words shift the order of her thoughts. Then she flings out a hand for me. "Draven…"

I turn my back and walk away. The ache in my chest grows heavy and sits on top of my lungs. Closing my eyes, I walk towards the barn. After a moment, her fur-lined boots scuff in the snow. She is likewise walking away from me. The ache in my chest travels up my throat where it seems content to sit.

Though I know she is gone, I feel as if Victoria is laughing at me.

The barn is empty. Willow hasn't yet arrived. I'm about to take a seat on the dirt floor beside the sleeping hens on their roost when the door creaks. I spin around, my hunting knife unsheathed before I even have time to think.

A cloak. A red cloak. Another girl. Willow.

"Sorry," she whispers.

I lean against the side of the barn as the startled energy flees my frame. I close my eyes. My bees are buzzing now.

Willow's fingers gently wrap around my wrist. She takes the knife out of my hand and slides it back into its sheath. "We don't have to go tonight."

I open my eyes. Of course. She must have passed Megan on the path.

Her. When Megan said "her," she meant Willow.

So much is happening at once. It's as if my thoughts are hitched to the bees, darting and buzzing about. I rest my hand on Willow's wrist in thanks then step past her for the door.

Yes, it will be tonight. How is tonight different than any other night?

My throat tightens. I know I have hurt Megan. I'll miss her smiles. Her tallness in every way. But I am not whole.

Willow trails behind me, hugging the cloak to her body. We enter the woods in silence. Several minutes pass before my thoughts calm enough for me to notice that I'm several yards ahead of Willow, as if she isn't even there. I stop where I am and wait for her. She casts me the faintest look of appreciation as she catches up.

We continue towards the river, side by side, without speaking. Two owls call to each other in the cold. Haunting voices, echoing into the moonlight.

"It is strange," Willow softly begins, "how accustomed we have become to the dark. Sometimes it's the daylight that feels foreign. But this..." She peers at the boughs around her from beneath her red hood that looks browner in the moonlight. "This is somewhat comforting. Familiar."

"It is," I softly agree.

We pick our way over a fallen pine. Her foot gets stuck on the cloak that is too big for her so I give her my hand and help her over the debris. Then we continue. I feel her gaze on me and it only makes my throat ache more. I don't know why. I don't know why. Perhaps because she's here with me in the woods, in the middle of the night.

"You are quiet, Draven."

I shoot her a surprised look that is more of a glare than I intend. I'm always quiet. Why should she care now, after all these years?

Her face softens apologetically. "And comely. It would be easy for someone to fill that quietness with their own thoughts. To see in you whatever best suits their needs."

My neck and cheeks are suddenly blazing. She knows.

"You heard." I can't hold her gaze. I focus on brushing aside branches as we walk.

Her voice is hesitant. "You weren't at the barn. I came to your window to wake you and... I didn't mean to overhear but..."

"You are good at listening."

I should mind that she listened. That she hid in the shadows. Instead, all I can think about is the madness of having two young women planning on rapping on my window in the same night. It's so ridiculous that I let out a low chuckle. That chuckle turns into a laugh. I can feel the tension in Willow increasing at my side over my odd reaction.

"I just walked away," I say at the end of a laugh, shaking my head. "His name is Draven and he is a craven."

Willow snatches my arm and spins me around to face her so quickly that I nearly lose my footing. "*Never*," she seethes, "speak of yourself that way again."

Her expression completely silences me. She is livid. I've never seen her so angry with me before in my life. I can't move.

"You are *not* a coward," she continues. "You are so very, very far from a coward."

The tightness in my throat increases. My bees are humming with a cadence I have never before heard. Something is growing in me. Something like the shout only quieter. More painful.

"Then why did I let her..." I gasp. But the words are gone. There are none for what I want to say.

Willow's lips grow thin as she presses them together for a moment, looking like her mother when scolding Jasper, before she speaks. "If you already miss her this terribly then go see her in the morning. You live on opposite sides of Morrot, that's all. It isn't as if one of you is dead and the other is left alive."

"You said she was dead," I whisper.

Willows eyes narrow as she studies my face. She parts her lips to ask who so I continue for her.

"She *was* dead. Just a... body. Just a body smaller than mine and yet I let her..."

My throat is so terribly tight. I look away from Willow's eyes, trying to find a space to breathe but there is nothing but Victoria surrounding me.

"I let her touch me," I whisper to the silvery tree trunks. "I let her kiss me." The trees blur. My eyes are moist. I turn them back onto

Willow who is still holding onto my arm, her grip tighter. "I let her take from me. I let her take so much."

"Oh, Draven." Her gaze darts to the scar on my neck. "She took from all of us."

I shake my head, tugging my arm out of her grip just to place my palm over the scar, hiding it from her view.

"No. No, I spoke with her. Was... was seduced by her."

A cough escapes that is half of a sob. It shifts the tears in my eyes to my lashes as I force myself to hold onto Willow's gaze, despite the rawness of the words as they come out.

"Willow, she almost had everything before I refused her. *That's* what I let her do."

My heart thuds in my ears. Willow gazes at me with a pinch between her fair brows. Her own eyes seem to glisten in the moonlight. Her lower jaw trembles the slightest bit. I wait, giving her room to speak, but she doesn't. Not a word. Because she knows the truth now and I have disgusted her.

"I am a coward," I continue softly. "And now she is in every touch. Every desire." My hand falls away from my scar. "I am marked. I am so terribly marked."

Willow shakes her head the slightest bit, her brow relaxing. "This has changed you. There is no going back."

I'm about to nod in agreement when she continues.

"That is what you said to me after Scarlet died. Because you, too, felt it after you lost your father. I *am* changed because of Tristan. And now you are changed because of Victoria." Her eyes seem as if they're blazing as she closes the distance between us. "But you did not 'let' her do anything to you, Draven. You did not approve or allow or consent. It happened and you were beguiled. Injured. Overpowered. There was no 'let.'" She takes a deep steadying breath, her eyes clearing from any tears. "Victoria did what she has always done. She took without permission."

"I could have struggled more," I insist. "Fought."

"There was nothing to fight," she hisses. "Believe me, I tried."

I shake my head, the tightness in my throat so unbearable that more tears are marring my vision. "Why?" I whisper.

Something in Willow breaks and she suddenly looks so small. "Because of me. You were only there because of me. She only used you to get to me. It's my fault, Draven, and I am so sorry for the weight you now carry."

"No," I groan as my tears drop from my lashes. "No, Willow, this isn't your fault. This isn't your fault."

"Of course it is," she insists, a puff of her exhale illuminated in the moonlight. "She knew who you were before you even made it to the house because she had heard me talking about you. She lured you there. How could it not be my fault? How could it not be when—"

"Because I would have come anyway," I shout over her.

Willow blinks at me in surprise. My torso trembles and my bees are quiet, as if even they are startled by my outburst.

"If I had known you were there all that time, I would have come in a heartbeat."

"Draven…" she whispers. There's something about her face that is pulling my insides to the surface.

"I looked for you," I continue, my voice firm. "Every day. Even when I thought I was only going to find a body. So if I ever had any inkling that you were in that place, I would have come for you, Willow. I would have come for you and I still would."

She is on the brink of tears, her eyes pulling more and more out of me. She is so still. So very still.

"*Nothing* that happened is your fault," I repeat, latching onto the fabric of her cloak. "How could it be when I would make the same choice even now, when I know *exactly* what I will find in that house?"

As she holds my gaze with her shimmering eyes, I realize what it is about her face that is so pulling on me. It's her plainness.

Willow is not beautiful. She's as familiar as my childhood blankets. As agreeable as quietness. Willow is not beautiful because she is radiant. A light in the darkness. A warmth in the cold. Willow is not beautiful because she is my heart outside of my body and I love her. I always have. Not in the wild, passionate way people loved in Scarlet's stories. Not with the swiftness for which she fell for Tristan. Instead, I love her with the steadiness of a tree. Deep roots and a tall, slow-growing trunk, reaching for the sky. The sun. The stars. I love her like the woods and the fresh earth. The new grass and the warm breeze. I love her like the sunlight and the darkness. I love her like the salmon in the river and the falcon in the sky: free.

I don't know if she reads any of this in me. How could she? How could she when I cannot even speak it in words? But there's something so terribly deep inside of her, pulling all of this out, that I realize I may not need to say it, after all. She knows. The wretched grief and longing in her gaze tells me that she has always known.

The wetness of my tears is chilling the skin beneath my eyes. I hope she isn't cold, for here in the snow, we have cracked the silence that lay between us for so terribly long. I'm lighter for it. Because no matter what happens now, no matter that we are both still limping along inside, we have blazed a path in the unchartered territory between us. A path to each other. It's not a new thing, it was just over-grown. And it will wait for us. There's no rush to take the first step. Perhaps we already have.

"The house," Willow whispers, looking away to wipe at the tears in her lashes with her cloak. "You saw your Watcher outside the house."

I nod, panting as I slowly descend into the moment again.

"You said she pointed in its direction?"

"Yes," I whisper, repressing a shudder over the ghoulish image of the woman on the brink of a scream.

"Then maybe she wasn't luring you at all. Maybe she was warning you."

With a sniffle, I take a moment to collect myself then peer about in the woods, having forgotten where we were. The river is not too far off. I take a step towards it and Willow follows. I don't know why this woman who died so long ago would be warning me. Watching me. I struggle to shift my mind back to her.

"Let us ask the bones."

# Chapter Eighteen

We arrive at the place where I last saw the Watcher. The alder trees keep their vigil over the remains. Crouching, I tug out the contents of my bag and use the flint and steel to light the rush-light. Willow studies the bones in the golden rays, frowning slightly.

"What do you need?" I ask.

"I don't know."

I set the light down in a pocket of snow, wedged in some rocks. Willow surveys the area then clears away some of the snow. She drops into a sit and cocks her head, concentration lines on her face. Something's in her hands, and after a moment I realize it's the strip of fabric. She closes her eyes and turns the cloth over in her fingers.

Easing down into a crouch, I wait. I know this may be fruitless. Bidding the dead to come forth is a new skill for Willow. Nothing may happen at all.

The owls continue their conversing around us as Willow's face relaxes. Two branches squeak together. I peer upwards. The naked branches of the alders are dingy silhouettes in the moonlight. They hiss with the breeze.

"Come to me," Willow whispers, redirecting my attention to her. "Come to me, Watcher. Come to me."

She continues to turn the piece of cloth over in her hands. Sometimes she is silent. Other times, she whisper-bids the spirit to come forward. My legs went numb long ago but I'm not tired.

More minutes pass. Then even more. I'm about to change positions and drop into a sit when a gust of wind makes the rushlight flicker. Willow is nearly cast into darkness. Reaching over, I cup the flame to shield it as I pick it up. I use my body to protect it from the wind. The golden light returns, dancing on Willow's face. And something else.

I slowly turn my head. The Watcher is standing just outside of the ring of shifting light. Her white dress covers her tall frame and her brown hair rests loose on her shoulders. Though most of her face is still in shadow, I can see enough to know that she is gazing at Willow.

"She is here," Willow whispers, the serene expression never leaving her face.

Though everything in me is stiff, I do my best to keep from moving either away from or towards the spirit. This ought to feel strange. Frightening. Instead, it's only awkward. But I am cautious all the same. I don't want the Watcher stepping any closer to Willow. After Victoria, a spirit will never be *just* a spirit again.

Willow holds her head to the side, as if leaning in to a whisper. "Lydia. Her name is Lydia." A line forms between Willow's brows and her face flushes with focus. Then she parts her lips and lets out a small gasp.

Alarmed, I peer up at the Watcher, surprised to find her gazing upon me instead. She takes a small step into the light. I don't tense as I ought to. Willow lets out another soft sound but I can't look her way because for the first time, I can see my Watcher's face.

It is soft. Her eyes are a deep, dark brown. Almost black. And she's gazing at me with a smile of such affection that I want to go to her. She is tall, slender and beautiful in a very simple way. And she calls to me. Something shimmering in her very essence fills me with a warmth I have never before felt. It takes almost everything in me to stay where I am.

But I can't help myself. She needs me. So I stop sheltering the rushlight. I reach out a hand. The Watcher's smile only grows and I feel my own begin in return. She bends down slightly, reaching out her hand for mine. We must touch. I need her touch. It is safety and warmth and now only an inch from my fingers.

Then the unprotected light is snuffed out. I feel nothing.

"Draven?" That's Willow's voice. It's alarmed.

Blinking, I jerkily grab my flint and steel. I relight the rush. The golden hue is again in the air. The Watcher is gone.

"No," I gasp, twisting and holding out the light, searching for her in the surrounding woods.

"Draven."

She is nowhere to be seen. I pivot to peer behind me and almost fall over.

"*Draven.*"

Willow's voice is firm. I face her, giving her all of my attention. Tears stain her cheeks. Her expression is odd. A mixture of confusion and fright. She parts her lips to speak then seems to think better of the words she has chosen.

"Willow," I softly plea, "who is she?"

Willow blinks but holds my gaze. "Your mother."

Willow and I sit at the base of an alder, huddled together for warmth. The rushlight isn't nearly as bright as it was when the spirit was here. I don't know how much time has passed since she left. Time has no real meaning anymore. I'm lost in my own mind.

Mother.

A dead woman is my mother.

Not Gwen. Not Lucian's wife. Not the only woman I have ever known as my mother. No, she *is* my mother. She must be.

Willow wept for some time. I didn't ask any questions. I knew she would give me the answers when she was ready.

"She is powerful," she whispers with the tiredness of tears muffling her voice, even though she has stopped crying. "I could almost... I could almost see everything she was telling me."

I scoot a little closer, though not completely from the cold. Willow eyes me as I do so.

"She kept saying the same thing at first. Like some sort of nursery rhyme and I worried that she had lost her intelligence. Like the spirits that walk up and down halls every night. They're just echoes. She said that you are the rabbit's—"

"The rabbit's child," I softly interject, my gaze lost in the shifting flame of the rush in tallow. "The acorn and the thistle down."

Willow cocks her head. "You could hear her?"

"I have heard it before."

"Where?"

Were she anyone other than Willow, I wouldn't answer. But she isn't. "The trees."

"What do you think it means?" she croaks.

I meet her reddened gaze and can't fight off the twinge of concern as I take in her wretched state on my account. "Why did you cry?"

Willow takes a deep breath, her eyes slowly becoming unfocused and drifting away from mine as she retreats into her memories. "Because sometimes spirits linger, not because they are afraid or malicious, like Victoria... but because they have loved so very fiercely."

"She loved me?" I whisper.

She closes her eyes. "Yes."

I press my side into hers and Willow rests her head on my shoulder.

"That's why I could see her," I muse. "She is family."

Willow shifts to peer at the remains a few feet from us. An eye socket of the skull is peeking out of the snow. "You were born from those bones."

The thought makes me feel like a wind in a canyon. Like an echo. I wrap an arm around her waist.

"I can't make sense of it all," Willow continues. "That nursery rhyme kept interrupting and nothing was in order. But Lydia is from a city in the south, like Tristan was. She was unmarried when she became with child. She was hidden away, or she hid herself away until you were born. Her family wouldn't help her, so she took you north. She traded everything she had for supplies. Just her and a baby and a mule. An unmarried woman and a baby would be unwelcome most everywhere, but she had heard stories about mountain villages. Places where a person could disappear. She was determined. Very determined."

"She almost made it," I whisper. I cannot imagine making such a journey south, let alone a single young woman with an infant coming north. Even if she had reached Morrot, Elias would have turned her away, or worse.

Willow nods. "She was camped somewhere in our valley. It was the summer after a hard winter. Everything was hungry. You crawled out of her arms in the middle of the night. She awoke to the laughing of coyotes. One was luring you away from the campfire. Lydia charged and chased it off, but another came from behind, then another. They were nipping at you and you were crying."

As I stare at the rushlight flame, I see it as the remains of Lydia's campfire. The baby is being harassed by the canines, the same way songbirds will dive and peck at a raiding crow.

"Then one attacked her," Willow continues. "She fought with the only weapon she had: her hands and feet. She scratched and clawed and hit and kicked. The coyotes fled but she was injured. Her leg was a mess. She bound it and continued anyway. Then she got sick. Everything hurt. She couldn't think. She ran out of milk. She lost all sense of direction and though she was parched, she couldn't stop drooling."

My stomach tightens. Willow knows this illness as well as I do. We call it the Fear of Water. People get it from wild animals. Once it sets in, there's no stopping it. The sick person or animal can no longer drink.

I've seen a deer with it before. I had thought I was just an incredibly stealthy hunter because the stag let me get so close. Then I saw the drool. I barely escaped being gored by climbing a tree. When an animal gets the Fear of Water, even prey can attack. The thought of Lydia suffering from such a disease makes me clench inside.

"She was bitten while protecting me," I say aloud.

Willow wraps an arm around mine, hugging it while her head continues to rest on my shoulder. She is quiet for the length of several heartbeats before speaking again.

"She wandered away from the mule and the supplies. She got lost. One night she thought she could smell smoke, so she set out with you towards it, looking for help. She collapsed and knew that she couldn't ever get up. You were crying so she curled up around you to keep you warm. To keep you safe from the coyotes. Then she died."

The strip of white fabric now sitting on Willow's knee flutters softly. The idea of my birth mother stumbling around in nothing but a smock, half crazed... knowing that someone I can't even remember died for me makes me feel as if I have lived the most luxurious life.

"Did Lucian find me," I ask, "when he was out hunting?"

"I don't know. I only know what Lydia could share, and she was dead by then."

We both grow quiet. It sounds as if it's starting to rain, but it's snow. Willow and I lose ourselves in watching the snowflakes for some time before I speak.

"I am the rabbit's child. The acorn and the thistle down." Taking a deep breath, I let it out slowly. "When do you ever see a baby rabbit?"

Willow is quiet as she thinks then speaks, realization coloring her voice. "When they are abandoned."

"Like the acorn and the thistle down," I muse. "Foundlings left to find their own way."

Willow shifts to peer at me and I feel her absence from my side with a small shiver. "Only she didn't abandon you, Draven."

I meet her clear, sea-green gaze.

"She fought for you until her last breath, and then she continued to try to protect you. To guide you. To watch over you."

The tightness is returning to my throat and I'm so exhausted that I don't know if I can bear it.

"She gave you your name. Draven. It means 'the child of beautiful shadows.'"

Everything in me cracks but I have done enough crying tonight. I fold in on myself, shutting out the world. Willow hugs my side. My breathing comes in sputtering and stuttering, tearless gasps. The bones of my mother are at my feet. I stepped on one without ever knowing. She tried to warn me about Victoria, the other spirit. She appeared to me because she wanted to watch me grow. And I never knew. All along, she was just an oddity. An apparition. Not the source of my life in every way possible. Not my loving mother. Love.

Willow rubs my back. "I am here, Draven. And you are made of the most beautiful shadows I have ever seen."

I lean in to her as the snow falls around us.

When we return to my home, I hesitate at the door. Willow reads the question in my eyes. There's straw in the barn from this autumn's meager harvest. We slip inside and burn the remainder of the rush-light. Willow uses her cloak as a blanket for the pair of us as we curl up beside each other. She hugs my back, wrapping an arm around my torso and I hold it there, watching the cloud of my breath and the dancing of the light and shadows on the inside of the barn.

"We watched Lady grow up here," I whisper.

Willow is quiet. I wonder if she's asleep. Then she laughs softly. "It took forever."

My quiet chuckle joins hers.

The following morning, my mother empties the trunk in her room. As she does so, I remember the piece of a saucer that I found on the day that I fell into the river and now regret not keeping it, wondering if it was one of Lydia's supplies. At the bottom of the trunk, my mother pulls out a thin, tattered green blanket. Her expression is tight as she lays it on the table in front of me and Willow. She folds down a corner to reveal dark stitching. A name. *Draven.*

"You were never any less my son," she croaks around unshed tears.

I trace a finger over the needlework, hoping that it was done by Lydia's hand, then rise and hug my mother. "I know, Mama," I soothe, rubbing her back. "I know."

Behind us, Willow gently unfolds the blanket.

# Chapter Nineteen

I never ask why my parents never told me the truth. I already know why. I was odd enough without the added strain of knowing that I was a foundling. Without fretting over who birthed and sired me. After all, I had parents.

The only thing my mother tells me is that no one else knows. She wasn't often in town anyway so she faked a baby bump once I was discovered by my father. Pretended that she had just hidden it well in the beginning. I didn't grow up in town, so no one ever noticed how old I was when they finally met me.

Megan avoids me for the rest of the winter. She offers me polite smiles when passing but that's all. Her hair grows in nicely and I'm happy for her. Willow plays with Jasper more and more. She only accepts visits from those wishing to contact the dead on certain days of the week.

At the first sign of spring, I begin wandering. I'm on the hunt for something special. I find it the same day that the ground thaws enough to bury my mother's bones in Morrot's cemetery. It's a hawk's nest with three eggs. The parents will never be able to raise three chicks. One will be pushed out of the nest by the others. It will drop to the ground like an acorn or thistle down. I carefully collect the egg from the nest at the top of a dead fir, keeping it upright, then tuck it into my tunic and climb down.

There is no accident this time. No almost fall with rope burns on my hands. I'm much older now, after all. I wrap the hawk egg in my father's finest otter pelt all the same and slip it under a broody hen in the night. By the time the first blooms have begun to open, I have a scrawny, downy chick.

Willow comes by when she can to see him. I rest a hand on her back when she holds him and she touches me when she laughs. The unchartered territory between us grows smaller and smaller with each smile.

She is Willow and Willow is my friend.

By the time my hawk can fly, I know what I want to call him. But I must ask permission first. And make a confession that I have kept for far too long.

Willow joins me in Elias' library one late spring afternoon. I don't like to come into the place. The only other time I have been inside wasn't a pleasant memory. Most of the books and scrolls have been returned to their shelves, but there are a few stragglers. No one is left in Morrot who knows how to read, so I have no idea if Willow and I are putting them in the correct place.

"I hope you don't mind," I say after several lengths of silence.

She shoots me a questioning glance. Her freckles are already back. I use my eyes to gesture to the walls surrounding us.

"Scarlet."

Instead of withdrawing, Willow smiles and pauses to peer around the room. "I like to think of her here. She loved these books. Even though she has moved on beyond the Netherworld, I can..." She closes her eyes and takes a deep breath of the odd scents of paper and parchment and dust. "I can feel her here."

Oh, how very much you have healed and bloomed, Willow.

"I think she would like that," I softly reply.

The Netherworld.

"Willow..." I hesitantly begin, tracing my fingers over the gold shapes on the spine of a tome that I know are letters to the trained eye. "There is something else Tristan said when I saw him when I was sick."

She fixes her full attention on me at the sound of his name. Though I am reluctant to, I meet her gaze.

"He... he had a choice."

Willow gently takes the book from my hands and places it on the shelf at her side. "I know," she softly replies.

I watch her with puzzlement as she glances around the room, peering for anything left out of place, as if I hadn't just revealed a barbed secret.

"You know?"

She doesn't flinch as she meets my gaze. "I know that he wouldn't linger. Not after our goodbyes were said." She sucks in a deep breath which is the only revelation of how difficult this actually is for her. "He wanted me to dance. To laugh. He wanted me to live. Not to be chained to his spirit like Victoria did to him." Though she smiles again, her lips are trembling. "He wanted me to keep saying hello."

Maybe it's the emotion she is trying to control, or the memory of Tristan's immense generosity, but I find it hard not to feel a tug in my own throat. I swallow past it all the same.

We leave the library behind and step out into the sunlight.

"He was a wonderful person," I observe. Willow turns to face me. "He gave so freely, despite his hardships. He helped you save my life, and I would be... It would be a privilege to name my hawk after him. In honor of him and... and both of you. What you shared." I have to swallow again past the tightness. "What you *share*."

Willow studies me for the length of several heartbeats. I'm worried that I have offended her. That she will not want to hear his name so often. For it to be associated with an animal and not a man.

Instead, she once again smiles past the strain in her eyes. "That would be the greatest gift of all."

Spring eases into summer and with Tristan now able to fly, I feel as if can, as well. No walls can contain me. No duties can keep me from the forests and all of its shifting shades of green. My mother laughs at my appetite and my rediscovered love of climbing trees, telling me that I am in a second childhood. It's just as well. After all, what is childhood other than a time of growth and learning? A time of exploring and playing and letting your veins fill with wonder.

I have nightmares about my time ill in bed. About being too weak to move. A prisoner of my own body. But I'm healed now. Not only from my illness but from food. My trousers and tunics again fit as they should. If anything, I'm growing thicker than I used to be.

Sometimes I race Tristan by launching him in the air then sprinting beneath him across meadows and through groves. I run until my legs and lungs burn. Until my blood boils so hot and swift that I have to dunk into streams. Tear my tunic off. Lie in the dewy grass and catch my breath in the shade.

There was a time, not long ago, even after I recovered, when it felt impossible to ever feel this good again. To ever be filled with such delight, despite every scar. Every memory and every loss. I am quick to laugh because I'm alive and so are my mother and Willow and Jasper and Cavan. I am ready to smile because there are green and growing things all around me. And I'm ready to love because it is what I was made to do.

So I love everything. My family. Tristan. The alders and the owls. The mosquitos and the cattle and the scent of their fertilizing dung. I love my mother's wrinkles and the stink of Jasper's unwashed hair and the way Cavan smiles at me as if I were Jasper's brother. Maybe I am. For Cavan feels like both father and an equal to me. We hunt together and dine together and Willow can serve my mother bread. Can see her as the woman she is, not the deeds she has done.

If Willow can forgive, then we all can.

Megan tells everyone that she's going to keep her hair short but seems to be letting it grow in anyway. I pretend I believe her because I like her defiance and she knows it. Though it took the better part of the winter for her to come around to speaking to me again, she's now a good friend.

There will always be a sort of question between us. Something left unanswered. But it was all about the wonder, anyway. It's the question that keeps us talking. We both know the answer would likely drive us apart in the end.

She opens up a storefront in the village and sells her baked goods. People stop talking about her as Megan the miller's daughter. She is now Megan the baker. It may sound quaint to outsiders, but fewer professions are more highly valued by a mountain community that once nearly starved to death.

I know I am talked about, as well. And Willow. She is called the Breaker of Darkness. People look to her as much as they look to me for advice. Usually more so, for I will always be Draven Who Does Not Speak. My bee-letters will always be skittish around strangers and stress. But I don't mind anymore. For the first time in my life, people are patient with me. They smile with me, because it isn't all about words. It's about connecting. Sharing. Words are only a small part of that.

Megan tells me that I'm called Draven the Just. I don't mind it. Not for the way that they mean it, but because of the word 'just.' I can flip it in my mind to be Just Draven.

I don't tell anyone outside of Willow's family about Lydia. My mother never says a word about this choice but I can tell she is relieved. She knows I'm her and Lucian's son. Nothing will ever change that. But I also came from the bones in the forest.

I have not seen the spirit of my mother since that night in the snow and the rushlight. Perhaps she has been waiting all of these years for a chance to tell her tale but never wanted to use her strength to communicate with Willow. Strength that she could use instead to show herself to me. To let me know that I was never a foundling and never alone. It's odd to feel so indebted, so thankful for a person I cannot even remember, but I know she's there all the same. For it is not only fear and greed that can bond a spirit, but love and sacrifice.

My Watcher. I hope she watches me live the best life I possibly can.

I no longer try to dig out Willow's roots in my heart or nip the buds of hope. They make me feel good. To breathe and run and swim in hope, to blow out candles and touch bones and bind wounds in hope is the closest I have ever felt to soaring, and we all deserve to soar. After all, this is our one life. We must barrel into it with abandon.

I didn't learn this on my own. Willow has been a bloom in her own right. She sings with Jasper. Invites me to camp outs where we build a fire in the field beside her cabin and roast sausages then the three of us sleep under the stars. Well, sleep as much as we can with Jasper tossing and turning between us and stealing the quilt.

The sadness that used to cling to her every other thought has faded to the fringes. It's still there in the corners of her eyes when she is caught by surprise by Tristan's memory. But she speaks of him now with a fond smile. I'm amazed by how quickly they grew together. As if they clashed and cracked each other open. I could never crack like that. Pour myself into someone I have only just met. But Willow can. She could, and I'm glad that we are different.

There's a push and a pull to our friendship that wasn't there before. Or maybe I just notice it more now in the light. Any tension is welcome and warm, even when it's stemming from an argument over how to respond to a villager's need or what kind of dog Jasper ought to ask for on his birthday. Tension means life. Two things moving together as much as they are moving apart. But moving apart doesn't always have to mean in opposite directions.

Victoria's grip on me is fading. I am able to think of her now as a deranged woman, not a force I was unable to stop. I was no one to her but a plaything. A tool. A body. It's both difficult and easier to know that she felt no closeness with me. That her lust was never about me at all.

Sometimes Willow hugs me. She flings her short frame at my abdomen or back. I used to stumble and laugh, caught off guard. I used to grow tense even without wanting to. But now I don't lose my footing. I relax and hold her. Because I'm safe and so is she. We are safe in each other. Though she is strong on her own and I am sensing my own firmness in my being, we lose nothing by gifting that strength to each other whenever we can.

This morning we took Jasper and Tristan with us into the woods to a meadow by the stream. I tossed my hawk into the air, knowing there were mice about, but Tristan only wanted to circle and drift on the warm currents above us. I can't blame him for it's a pleasant, warm day.

Jasper asked me to help him look for gold in the creek so we left Willow lying in the soft grass, enjoying the sun that has turned her skin a deep shade of gold. I don't tell the boy who is now a good inch taller than he was last winter that gold is very difficult to find. Instead, I help him hunt in the shallows.

On my wrist, so very green against the chestnut of my skin, is the braided grass of a bracelet Willow made for me. The first in months. I'll be careful that Tristan's talons don't shred it when I call him back to me.

Jasper grows bored and aimlessly plunks a rock into the water. I notice a trove of flat, round stones, perfect for skipping, and crouch to collect them. Jasper watches as I toss one into the deeper portion of the creek, skipping it once, then hand another to him. He gives it a try but the rock merely makes a splash. The next rock makes an even louder plunk. When he lets out a giggle, I realize that he isn't trying to skip them at all anymore. This is a game. I chuck mine in so hard that it sprinkles him with cold.

The challenge has been set. I lock eyes with the boy half my height, shoving away the memory of how I used to so fret about his survival. Carry him to conserve his energy. I shove these memories away not because they are unimportant, but because they don't serve me now, and *now* is where I am.

I make the first move, darting into the water and bending to scoop up a handful. Jasper squeals and does his best to run through the ankle-deep river, trying to get far enough upstream to escape my splash, but there is no escape. His peal of laughter as the cold water strikes him makes mine tumble out, as well. Soon he's spraying me back like a dog digging a hole. I can't stop laughing at the sight of him.

Then I take a misstep and my boot slips on a slimy rock. I land hard enough to know that I'll have a bruise tonight but I cannot be distracted by the pain. Not when Jasper is launching towards me.

"Charge!" he crows.

He's joined by a blur of light blue. A dress. Willow is suddenly in the water, assisting Jasper in his quest to soak me. Rising to my knees, I sweep my arm in the water to spray them both. Willow squeals and the two attempt a clumsy retreat. I rise and trot after Willow, who is laughing so hard that she can't even tell me to stop and to go after her brother instead.

I hook my arm around her waist and throw myself down where the bottom is sandy. Her scream is full of delight as she lands on my chest, her hand on my wrist beside the bracelet. Somewhere upstream, Jasper is belly laughing.

Willow peers down at me, her wet hair dripping onto my sodden shoulders, her freckles all the darker against her golden skin. The water is hardly any warmer than icemelt. We are surrounded by cold and yet we are warm. Her weight is a comfort, her sea-green gaze a boon, her laugh a honey.

Honey. The bee-letters in my breast hum softly making such sweetness.

Her laughter fades into a smile as she reaches out to drag a stray lock of yellowed hair off of my brow. Willow's thumb drags across the scar on my neck then rests on my shoulder. Her eyes upon me are as the spring. I am the spring.

In that moment, I know that the people of Morrot are wrong. She is not Willow the Breaker of Darkness. She is Willow, Bringer of Light.

And I...

I am Draven Lucian's Son. I am the one who has been seen.

# Acknowledgments

Thank you to my wonderful family and friends who have always believed in me and encouraged me to follow my inner voice and flourish. I have come a long way since the girl voted the "quietest in the 6th grade"!

Special thanks is due to Tanya Christiansen. Her reader's eye sped this book along to fruition.

Last but certainly not least, thank *you*, dear reader, for investing a sliver of your life in this tale. May your path ever be charmed!

# About the Author

K.M. Rice is a national award-winning screenwriter and author who has worked for both Magic Leap and Weta Workshop. Her first novel, *Darkling,* is a young adult dark fantasy now available as an audiobook

Her novella *The Wild Frontier* is an ode to the American spirit of adventure and seeks to awaken the wildish nature in all of us. She also provided additional writing and research for *Middle-earth From Script to Screen: Building the World of The Lord of the Rings and The Hobbit.* Her upcoming *Afterworld* series is set to debut with the first book, *Ophelia.*

Over the years, her love of storytelling has led to producing and geeking out in various webshows and short films. When not writing or filming, she can be found hiking in the woods, baking, running, and enjoying the company of the many animals on her family ranch in the Santa Cruz Mountains of California.

*To find out more and join the wildling community:*

www.kmrice.com
kmriceauthor@gmail.com

# More by K.M. Rice:

## NOVELS

- *Darkling*
- *The Wild Frontier*
- *The Country Beyond the Forests*
- *Afterworld Book I: Ophelia*

## AS A CONTRIBUTING AUTHOR

- *Middle-earth From Script to Screen: Building the World of the Lord of the Rings and the Hobbit*
- *Middle-earth Madness*

www.ingramcontent.com/pod-product-compliance
Lightning Source LLC
Chambersburg PA
CBHW020634250626
47154CB00008B/2678